THE RECKLESS WARRIOR

JENNIFER YOUNGBLOOD

ARBOR
HOUSE

MY GIFT TO YOU ...

Get Beastly Charm: A Contemporary retelling of beauty & the beast as a welcome gift when you sign up for my newsletter. You'll get information on my new releases, book recommendations, discounts, and other freebies.

Get the book at:

http://bit.ly/freebookjenniferyoungblood

1

All in all, it had been a productive day, despite the disastrous beginning. Delaney had put in ten long hours at the studio laying down tracks for the first song in her new album. Slowly but surely, she was making progress. The hard part had been pulling her mind away from the threatening texts and focusing on her work. Every minute counted these days. She had to have all six songs written and performed by the end of the month. *One down and five to go.*

Delaney leaned back against the seat of the car and let her mind get lost in the blur of lights from the city. Every inch of her body craved sleep. As soon as she got home, she was taking a hot shower and crawling into bed. Thankfully, she could sleep in a little in the morning before starting on the lyrics for her next song. The title of her album was "Transformation." She chuckled darkly. Transformation was a topic Delaney knew well. Maybe she should name her next song "Scratch and Claw." That's what she'd done—scratched and clawed her way to stardom despite all obstacles. But now that she was on the cusp of making it big, her past was catching up to her.

She fingered her neck, feeling like she had an invisible noose around it. She should've known her ex-husband Tuck would come lurking around when he realized she was on the verge of becoming a star. Sharks always came for the feed when they caught a whiff of fresh blood. An icy fear slithered down her spine as the all too familiar panic gripped her. Tuck wouldn't stop until he killed her.

Maybe she should've stayed out of the limelight. Even as the thought entered her mind, she knew that singing was nearly as important to her as breathing. She didn't want to spend the rest of her life hiding in the shadows, fearing each day that Tuck would return. Tuck and his brother had taken away everything else from her. She wouldn't allow them to steal this too. No matter what, she'd go down fighting. Her mind flitted over the recent events that had brought her to this point.

The first text came a little over a month ago, right after she made her first appearance on a popular late-night show. Her record label wanted to put her out there so that people would know Delaney Mitchell by the time her debut album came out. The plan was working. Delaney's Instagram and Twitter followers were doubling daily and she'd gotten a half-dozen requests to appear on several more well-recognized talk shows. Unfortunately, the notoriety put her on Tuck's radar.

Had she remained an obscure waitress, scratching out a meager income to get by, Tuck might've left her alone. But now that she was fast becoming *somebody*, he wanted a piece of the pie. No, what he wanted was a piece of her. In Tuck's warped mind, he believed he owned her like property he could abuse at will and then push aside until it suited his whim to pick it up again. She swallowed, glancing at the bulky outline of her bodyguard Mason's shoulders who was driving the car. It was good to know that she had someone with her always—a barrier that would hopefully keep Tuck from gaining personal access to her.

Immediately after receiving the first round of texts, Delaney had gone to the police and filed a restraining order against Tuck. Then she hired a service that would give her 24 hour, around-the-clock protection. It cost a pretty penny, but it was worth the peace of mind. Tuck and his family were from her hometown Noble, Alabama.

Although there wasn't anything noble about the one-horse town of her birth. She'd hoped that moving from Nashville to San Diego would help Tuck stay away. But she'd been fooling herself. After all, it wasn't like Tuck couldn't hop a plane.

Delaney changed her number and the initial texts had stopped. She'd hoped the ordeal was over. But this morning, it had started again. The text came through as she was wolfing down a bowl of cereal and getting ready to dart out the door for work.

Did you really think I wouldn't find you?

An hour later while she was at the recording studio surrounded by a team of musicians, another text came through. This one had her shaking.

You look good in those black jeans and turquoise boots.

And then ...

See you soon.

After the third text, she couldn't breathe. Tuck was here in San Diego, lurking somewhere nearby. He'd gotten close enough to see what she was wearing. Delaney rushed to the bathroom where she puked. Then she called her manager Milo Stanley. She was so panicked she could hardly talk, the words came out in strangled gulps as she slumped down against the wall and drew herself into a tight ball, rocking back and forth. Images from before burned through her mind ... Tuck taunting her, a tiger playing with its food before going in for the kill. The last time she saw him, he'd beaten her so badly that he'd put her in the hospital. Delaney figured Tuck experienced a moment of regret over his actions, which is why he agreed to a divorce. She went from the hospital to a home for battered women. The police came and took their reports but realized prosecuting Tuck was futile. Delaney was unwilling to testify against him. Not that she didn't want to see Tuck pay for what he did. But she was too afraid, not only of Tuck but of his older brother Hugh. She could see the relief in the officers' eyes ... knew they didn't want to tangle with the ruthless Allen brothers either. They thought nothing of going after police officers or anyone else who got in their way.

Her manager Milo helped calm her down. He said he was on his way to the studio and told her to call the police. At least the police force here wouldn't be cowed by Tuck. Two officers arrived to take her statement, then told her to call again if Tuck came anywhere near. "Tuck's just trying to scare you," Milo said. "You have highly skilled bodyguards surrounding you at all times. The closest Tuck can get to you is through texts."

"But how did he get this number?" Delaney wanted to know. "You said it was private."

"It is private," Milo countered. "Geez, Delaney, I don't know how he got it. But don't worry, we'll get you a new number."

Milo had spent a full hour talking to Delaney, trying to calm her down enough that she could get back to work. The record label had paid for studio musicians to come lay down tracks. The song had to be recorded today, or else the label would lose money. And that was unacceptable, especially for a new artist. Delaney was lucky Montana Crew's label agreed to produce her album. She couldn't risk messing things up.

So, she offered a few heartfelt prayers, asking for help. Then she drained several cups of black coffee and went to work. In a way, it was good to have something to focus on besides Tuck. Luckily, her persistence paid off. Nine hours later they finally had a quality product.

"Here we are, ma'am," Mason said politely as they pulled alongside the curb of her high-rise building. "Would you like for me to park the car and meet you inside your condo?"

"No!" The word came out more forcefully than she'd intended. She offered a strained smile to soften her rudeness. "We can use the valet service. I'd like for you to accompany me to my condo. Considering the texts ..."

Mason nodded, a deep crease forming in the center of his fleshy forehead. "Of course." He cocked his head looking thoughtful. "Miss Mitchell, if it makes you feel any better, it's highly unlikely that your ex could get past the front desk security in your building and then up to the tenth floor. You should be perfectly safe."

She suppressed a shudder. "Thanks," she mumbled, "but if it's all the same to you, I'd prefer if you go with me and do a check of my condo before I go in." While she appreciated Mason trying to ease her fears, he didn't know how ruthless Tuck was. It was better to be safe rather than sorry.

"Sure thing." Mason pulled up to the valet desk. As they got out, Delaney looked over her shoulder, her skin crawling. Was Tuck out there right now, watching her? She brushed aside the fear, straightening her shoulders. Something had shifted inside her today as she sat huddled on the bathroom floor, scared out of her mind. She felt small and pathetic ... at Tuck's complete mercy. Which is precisely how Tuck wanted her to feel. But enough was enough! Tuck Allen had caused her enough pain for ten lifetimes. If he came looking for her, he'd get the fight of his life.

THE FLOWING hot water helped soothe some of the tension from Delaney's aching shoulders. Her mind ran through possibilities for song lyrics, but it was hard to come up with anything since she was so tired. She dried off with a towel, then slipped on her robe. She was headed to her bedroom to put on underwear and pajamas when she heard a noise. She froze in her tracks, her heart picking up its beat. She cocked her ears.

Nothing.

She relaxed, laughing softly. This paranoia would be the death of her. Mason had done a thorough check of the condo, proclaiming it safe. And he was right outside the door where he'd be all night until his shift change when another bodyguard would take his place.

Delaney went to the dresser. She flinched when she heard a thump that sounded like someone was in the kitchen. Her throat constricted as she clutched her neck. For a second, she was unsure what to do. It seemed like overkill to call 911 because she heard a noise. She reached for her phone on the nightstand and stole into the hall. Her heart pounded out a ragged beat as she made her way to the kitchen. Had Mason come into the condo for some reason? She made a mental note to call the agency the following day and stipulate that under no circumstances were the bodyguards to enter her condo without her permission. If Mason needed something, he should've called.

"Hello? Mason? Is that you?" She stepped into the kitchen at the same instant she heard the grating laugh.

"Who the devil is Mason? That blockhead you had planted outside your front door?" A cruel grin twisted Tuck's handsome features, revealing the monster within. "Sugar, the next time you hire a bodyguard, make sure he doesn't have a weakness for a beautiful woman holding a box of doughnuts." He grunted. "The fool digested enough sleeping pills to keep him dozing for a good long time. Who knows? Maybe even enough to kill him."

The words flowed so casually out of Tuck's mouth, he might've been talking about the weather rather than the life of a human being. With his blonde hair, even features, and bright-blue eyes, Tuck was the quintessential golden boy—his outward appearance belying the psychopath within. He'd grown a mustache since she'd last seen him, and his hair was shorter.

She let out a cry, tremors shooting through her body. A wave of dizziness assaulted her as she staggered, trying to get her balance. Her mind tried to come to grips with the fact that her worst nightmare was sitting on a barstool, his feet propped on the kitchen island. An incredulous laugh rose in her throat. Tuck was munching on an apple, of all things. Her breath froze when she saw the pistol in his other hand. *Run!* her mind screamed. But to where? Tuck would shoot her before she made it two steps away.

She straightened her shoulders, trying to mask her fear with an expression of outrage. Tuck fed on weakness. "You have no right to be here."

"Oh, I have every right, darling." He looked her up and down, a brazen glint in his eyes.

Revulsion welled in her as she tightened the tie on her robe. "What do you want, Tuck?" She tried to think ... She was holding her phone. *Was it possible to call 911?*

"Did you really think you could get rid of me?" He laughed, but the coldness in his eyes sent shivers down her spine. "As if changing your stupid phone number or hiring a few bodyguards would keep me away." She felt like she was staring into the face of the devil as he locked eyes with her. Then his expression grew plaintive, like the child in him was taking centerstage. "I miss you." His voice grew pleading, confused. "H-how could you desert me? Your own husband?"

In the early days, she'd been taken in by Tuck's manipulation, believed there was good in him. It was a vicious cycle. He'd beat her senseless, then beg for her forgiveness, romancing her enough so that she'd actually believe things could be different. Then, when she let her guard down, the demon in him would rear its ugly head. Her voice sounded as brittle and hollow as she felt. "We're divorced, Tuck. You no longer have any claim on me."

He grunted. "Barbie Face, in the eyes of the Lord we're married 'til death do we part." His eyes narrowed. "The two of us will be together, until one of us is put in a box." His voice rose. "You got that?"

She jerked, hugging her arms. Wishing she could make herself small enough to disappear. Tuck had always called her *Barbie Face*. There was a time when she thought the nickname was cute. When she was young and stupid ... flattered that he noticed her.

Tuck tossed the half-eaten apple on the floor and sat up.

Delaney sensed a shift in his demeanor, knew everything was coming to a head. Tuck was tired of talking. Blood pounded against Delaney's temples. She tried to swallow down her alarm, keep her wits about her. "What do you want? Money? I'll give you as much as you want. Just leave me alone." She hated the desperate edge in her voice. Hated how small and miserable this man made her feel. Life with him had been a horrible series of memories that she wanted to erase from her mind.

His voice took on the silky tone of a snake, slithering around its prey. "Look at you … all high and mighty. Country music star Delaney Mitchell. Has a much better ring than Delores Millstead. But no matter how much lipstick you slather on a pig, it's still a pig, after all." He grunted. "To answer your question. I'll take the money and anything else I want." His eyes raked over her.

Revulsion welled in her stomach. She'd seen that look before, knew what it meant.

Tuck's voice took on a disinterested tone as he motioned. "Now take off that robe. It's time you performed your wifely duty."

Terror—swift and paralyzing—raced over her. And with that terror came a smoldering anger. It wouldn't be enough for Tuck to rape her, he wanted to humiliate her first. They'd been through this routine more times than she could count—her standing before Tuck while he pointed out all the flaws in her body like she was nothing more than a branded piece of livestock. It made her disgusted with herself that she'd allowed him to wield so much control over her.

"No!" Even if she died here tonight she wouldn't be subjected to his cruelty any longer.

His jaw went slack as he rocked back. Then he barked out an uncertain laugh before his eyes went hard. He swiped the glass fruit bowl with his arm, sending it flying to the floor where it splintered into pieces.

Delaney flinched, but held her ground. "Get out! Before I call the police."

Rage twisted Tuck's face as he sprang to his feet and rushed at her, knocking the phone out of her hand. He grabbed her throat and pushed her against the wall. She gurgled, trying to get her breath, her fingers clawing against his hand. Stars exploded before her eyes. In a matter of seconds, she'd pass out. A futile terror iced over her, her eyes bulging, her lungs craving air.

"You listen to me," he seethed, his face purple. "You belong to me! And you'll do what I say!" He released his hold on her throat. She coughed, drawing in a haggard breath. He pressed against her with his body weight, trailing the barrel of the pistol along her jaw. "Now whaddaya say we start this conversation over? The robe comes off!"

As he pulled at the tie, something inside her snapped. She let out a visceral scream and went on the attack, digging her fingernails into his eyes. Then she went for the pistol, trying to pry it out of his hands. No doubt, Tuck was stronger. Had she not taken him by surprise or been so enraged, she might not have stood a chance. But he stumbled back and tried to regain his balance. They wrestled, Delaney keeping a firm grip on the gun with both hands against his one hand. That was her only chance ... to get the gun away from him. Delaney heard a loud bang, felt the brunt kick of the gun being fired. For a split second, she thought she'd been shot.

No, not her.

Disbelief widened Tuck's eyes. "You shot me." He backed away, holding a hand over the wound in his torso as he slumped to his knees, then fell to the floor.

Delaney gasped, the hard reality of what had just happened overtaking her. Her body shook, her mind whirling. Somehow, she managed to get to her phone. She pressed 911.

"My ex-husband broke into my condo." Her voice broke. "I shot him." She looked at the blood pooling like an ink stain over his clothes. "I—I think I killed him." She dropped the phone and fell to her knees, sobbing.

A curious numbness came over Delaney as she stood in front of Tuck's hospital bed. He was in a coma, tubes hooked to his motionless body. She should feel grief, shouldn't she? She'd loved him once. But that love had been snuffed out, a bitter hatred filling the empty space.

No charges were being filed against her. It was a clear-cut case of self-defense. Tuck drugged her bodyguard, who thankfully was okay, and broke into her condo with the intent to rape and possibly murder her. While Delaney didn't have to worry about the legal repercussions, the media was having a heyday with the story. Milo was trying his best to do damage control for Delaney and the record label.

Milo was surprised and apprehensive when Delaney announced that she wanted to visit the hospital. He tried to talk her out of it, saying the press would be all over her. "The press will hound me regardless," she'd answered and could tell from the expression on Milo's face that he knew she was right.

Just as they suspected, Delaney had to fight her way through a throng of reporters camped near the entrance of the hospital. They shoved their microphones in her face and demanded answers, but she kept her eyes fixed forward and pressed through them. She needed to come here ... needed to put closure on the situation. According to the kind nurse who'd pulled Delaney aside and quietly relayed the information, Tuck's prognosis wasn't good. He'd lost a tremendous amount of blood, putting him into a coma. The doctors weren't sure if he'd ever regain consciousness.

How did Delaney feel about the news? Relief that Tuck could no longer hurt her? Sorrow for taking the life of someone she once loved? Maybe it was a combination of both.

She hugged her arms. "For what it's worth, I'm sorry," she said softly. "Sorry that it had to end this way." She paused, tears stinging her eyes. "But you hurt me. Took away my dignity." Her voice shook. "And I hate you for that."

"I always told Tuck you'd end up destroying him."

She whirled around. "H—Hugh?" She let out a shaky laugh, her hand going to her chest. "I didn't realize you were in town."

"Just got in this morning."

The icy look in Hugh's eyes caused a pit to form in her stomach. Unlike Tuck, Hugh didn't have a hot temper, but he was calculating and dangerous. The familial resemblance between the brothers was strong, except Hugh's face was blocky, his features craggy.

"Did you come to witness your handiwork?"

The accusation in Hugh's voice was a punch in the stomach. She rushed to explain. "Tuck broke into my condo with a gun. He tried to rape—"

"Save it," he snarled, holding up a hand. "That which happens between a man and his woman behind closed doors is none of my business."

She shook her head, disgust prickling over her. "And therein lies the problem. You've always turned a blind eye to Tuck, given him carte blanche to do whatever the heck he pleased. He was trying to rape me!"

A ruthless expression twisted Hugh's face, making him look inhuman. "Watch your mouth," he hissed.

She rocked back, alarm trickling over her. Hugh was a dangerous man, not one to tangle with.

He flashed a contemptuous smile. "I'm glad you're here so I can say this in person."

Her heart dropped. This couldn't be good.

He leaned forward, his voice barely over a whisper. "Whether you like it or not, you and Tuck are intertwined."

This was sounding like an eerie repeat of what Tuck had said.

"If he lives, you live. If he dies, you die."

She gasped, a roar starting in her ears. "It was an accident."

He just looked at her with a placid expression more terrifying than anger could've ever been.

A hysterical chortle rose in her throat. "You can't be serious. You're talking about murder."

"An eye for an eye," he said firmly.

This whole scenario was insane. Hugh was insane. She had to get out of here. She turned to flee the room. But before she could get out the door, she heard the leering amusement in Hugh's voice.

"Run little chickadee, run all you want. But know this. No matter where you go, I'll find you if the situation warrants. You have my word on that."

When Corbin approached the security guard at the gate of Sutton Smith's mansion he rolled down the window of his rental car.

"Your name, Sir?" the guard asked.

"Corbin Spencer."

The man's eyes trailed down the list. Then he nodded. "Have a nice evening."

"Thanks," Corbin said curtly as he continued to the mansion. It was in a private area of an exclusive section of Coronado Island, overlooking the San Diego Bay. Corbin had spent a handful of weekends here lounging by the pool and doing various other leisure activities, but never without Doug. His gut twisted as he thought about his best friend and fellow SEAL member, who'd been killed during a rescue mission in the Philippines when their platoon was ambushed. It had been seven months since Doug had passed, but tonight on the grounds of his estate the wound felt as raw as it had in the beginning.

When he reached the mansion, a valet attendant approached. "May I park your car, Sir?"

Corbin got out and tossed the keys to the attendant in exchange for a claim ticket. Then he smoothed down his white tuxedo jacket and adjusted the bowtie. He wasn't looking forward to the pretense of making small talk with a group of strangers at some party. And the worst part ... wearing this stupid monkey suit constricting his shoulders like a strait jacket.

Even though the event was black-tie, Corbin had planned to wear nice jeans and a sports jacket. But then, this afternoon, a tux was delivered to his room compliments of Sutton Smith. Too bad it was about a half size too small. Corbin couldn't wait to get back to the hotel to strip the thing off and put on jeans and a t-shirt.

He ran a quick hand through his spiky hair, figuring he was as ready now as he'd ever be. His gaze took in the sprawling English Tudor mansion. The only reason Corbin knew the architectural style was because Doug mentioned that his dad had brought in an English architect during construction to make sure the style was authentic. Sutton Smith's enormous wealth was staggering, and yet Doug had been so down-to-earth.

The place was brimming with high-society people dressed to the nines. As Corbin strode up the front steps, he thought back to the phone call that brought him here. Corbin was surprised to hear from his late friend's dad. He hadn't spoken to Sutton since Doug's funeral. At that time, Sutton was withdrawn ... angry at the world. Corbin didn't blame the man. He felt the same way about Doug's death.

Sutton opened the conversation by inquiring what Corbin was doing professionally. Then he extended an invitation to a gathering. Corbin grunted as he looked at the large staff of servers dressed in uniforms, scurrying to wait on guests. When he heard the word "gathering," Corbin assumed there might be twenty or thirty people present. But this was a full-fledged soirée with more people than he could count.

Corbin was currently living in Denver, Colorado and was short on funds. Before he could make up an excuse about why he couldn't attend the gathering, Sutton explained briskly that he'd already purchased Corbin a first-class ticket for the following day and booked him a room at The Luxe, a five-star hotel. Sutton went on to say that he had a proposition for Corbin and that he would pay him twenty-five hundred dollars for his time.

A free trip and an extra twenty-five hundred bucks were too good to turn down. Besides, Corbin's curiosity was piqued. He couldn't imagine what Sutton Smith wanted to talk to him about. He scoped the crowd, hoping to catch sight of Sutton. No luck.

He glanced at the string quartet off to the side, playing a merry tune. All around him, people were engaged in lively conversation. The air crackled with the excited hum of people enjoying themselves. The corners of his lips pulled down. There was nothing worse than being a loner in a crowd. Hopefully, he'd find Sutton soon.

"Would you like an appetizer?"

Delaney smiled politely before placing two spinach triangle pastries on her plate. "Thank you."

The server nodded and moved to the next guest.

It was too bad that Milo couldn't be here tonight. Then Delaney wouldn't feel so out of place. Milo had arranged her meeting with Sutton Smith, then realized that his girlfriend's son had the starring role in a school play. She sighed, taking a bite of the pastry. It was dryer than a chunk of sawdust. She coughed, trying to clear the crumbs from her throat. Now she needed a drink of water. She signaled to the closest server.

"How may I help you?" he said in a brisk, formal tone.

She touched her throat. "Could I get a glass of water?" *Before my windpipe closes off.*

"Certainly." He raised his hand and motioned to a girl across the room. She hurried to Delaney's side and gave her a glass.

Delaney took a few gulps. *Okay, no more pastries.* She glanced around the room, looking for a place to sit. When she first arrived and told the greeter her name, she was directed to an older lady who introduced herself as Agatha.

"Sutton is expecting you," Agatha said, "but he's tied up with guests. As soon as he's done, he'll find you. In the meantime, make yourself at home."

Delaney let out a long sigh. From the looks of things, it was bound to be a long night. She really couldn't complain though because she was just glad Sutton agreed to meet with her. Ever since Hugh had threatened her in the hospital, Delaney had been beside herself. Right after it happened, she called Milo, bawling so hard that she could hardly get the words out. He'd met her at a coffee shop, and she told him the whole sordid story. At first, Milo told her to go to the police. Then she explained how ruthless Hugh was and how she feared the police wouldn't be able to protect her against him.

Finally, Milo said he might have another option. Delaney had laughed out loud when that option turned out to be billionaire philanthropist, Sutton Smith. Then Milo told her a story about his girlfriend Leslie and how Sutton had saved her from her abusive husband Howie. But Sutton didn't stop there. He also gave Leslie money to pay for her son's leukemia treatments. Those treatments had saved the boy's life.

It was hard to believe that someone like Sutton Smith would do something so kind, asking nothing in return. Sure, he was a philanthropist. But most people like him simply donated money to charity and left it at that. Milo told Delaney that he would put out feelers, see if he could get in touch with Sutton and explain her situation.

The whole thing sounded farfetched, but Delaney was desperate enough to try anything. Fear was eating her alive. She had no doubt that Hugh would make good on his threat, and Tuck's prognosis wasn't looking good. The bullet wound had gotten infected. The doctors were amazed that he was still hanging on. Delaney had spent the last few days in a fog, hardly eating or sleeping. She'd tried to work, but it was impossible to get into a creative frame of mind with this hanging over her.

Even though Tuck had been so horrible to her, she didn't want to be responsible for his death. And then to add Hugh's threat into the mix, it was too much to deal with. She felt like she was on the verge of a mental breakdown. Prayer was the only thing keeping her functioning. She'd been praying every day for a miracle. And today, the dark curtain of clouds had parted for one tiny second, giving her hope that help might be around the corner.

Milo called this morning, telling her the good news. "Sutton agreed to meet with you at his estate. But he's having a party, so it'll have to be afterwards."

"I'll just wait and go after the party's over," Delaney had said.

"No, Sutton's assistant was adamant that you come to the party."

Milo couldn't remember the lady's name he spoke with, but Delaney was sure it was the older woman she'd met earlier ... Agatha.

The plate of uneaten pastries was starting to feel heavy in her hand. She didn't want to hold the blasted thing all night. She caught the nearest server. "Can I give this to you?" Her feet were aching. Why hadn't she worn lower heels?

The man nodded. "Of course. May I take your glass also?"

"I think I'll hold onto it. Thanks." It was one of those moments when Delaney was glad she was on the verge of hitting it big instead of a superstar like Dolly Parton or Montana Crew. It was good to still have some degree of anonymity. Of course at an event like this, most of the people were prominent and too preoccupied with their own importance to worry about Delaney's.

Absently, her mind wandered over the crowd. She caught sight of her bodyguard keeping a respectable distance. He gave her a slight nod as if to say, *I'm nearby, doing my job.* Her gaze moved to two middle-aged women engaged in an animated conversation. They were both so skinny they looked like skeletons, their faces stretched like plastic from so many cosmetic surgeries. Absently, she glanced toward the entrance as she took another sip of water. She nearly choked when she saw a man stride in, his angular jaw set firm like he owned the place. It had been a long time since she'd even noticed a man's appearance, much less found anyone attractive. Partly because she'd been too wrapped up in her career and mostly because the ordeal with Tuck had left her fearful about having a relationship. But she couldn't seem to peel her eyes away from this guy.

He had a rugged edge like he would've been more comfortable in casual clothes, although he certainly knew how to fill out a tux. He was a little over six feet tall with lean muscles—GI Joe on steroids. He walked with purpose, his eyes scoping the room like he was looking for someone. *It's me! I'm the one you're looking for.* She laughed at herself. Seriously? Where had that thought come from? The fact that she was even noticing a guy right now spoke to her frenzied emotional state. If Tuck didn't pull through, she'd soon be fleeing for her life. Her career would be snuffed out before it even got a chance to blossom. She'd have to go into hiding. And even then, Hugh would eventually find her. As bad as Tuck was, Hugh was a thousand times worse. He wouldn't think twice about taking her life, or anyone else's who got in his way. Her chest constricted, sweat beading across her nose. She balled her fist, willing herself to calm down. Hopefully, Sutton would be able to help. She had to keep her mind fixed on the hope of deliverance.

The guy's gaze connected with hers, sending a dart of warmth coursing through her veins. A slight smile tugged at his lips, and she felt herself smile back. The room shrank, all the people around her melting into a blur, and there was only him and her. Her heart hammered in her chest. He was coming her way. No! She couldn't do this! This guy would hurt her the same way Tuck had. Why was she always attracted to the wrong sort of man? This guy was tougher than nails, a rebel. She could tell from his swagger, the confident glint in his eyes.

She broke eye contact and quickly turned her back to him. She wasn't here to pick up on men. The fact that she'd felt so attracted to some random guy made her sick to her stomach. Hurriedly, she threaded through the people, intent on getting as far away from GI Joe as she could.

THAT WAS ODD ... the girl. Talk about hot and cold. One minute, she was giving Corbin a come-hither look, and the next, she was turning her back and running the other direction. He scowled. She was probably some high-society chic playing games. Too bad. She was stunning to look at. And for an instant, when their eyes locked, he'd felt a connection.

He threaded his way to the wall where he could observe the people in the room from a more inconspicuous place. Plus, he liked having his back protected. Still no sign of Sutton. Odd that he'd be MIA at his own party. Then again, there were so many people here, and the place was enormous. Sutton could be anywhere. He stood for another twenty minutes or so, still no sign of Sutton.

Finally, he got bored from being in the same spot and strode over to the bar and ordered a drink as he sat down at an open barstool. What must it be like to live a life of such grandeur? He thought of the modest cabin in the tiny town of Birchwood Springs, Colorado where his grandfather Pops and sister still lived. It was certainly a simpler life than this. And as far as Pops was concerned, the only way to live. Guilt tugged at him. It had been too long since he'd been home. He knew he should go back, but he couldn't handle thinking about Gram's situation.

The bartender returned with his drink. He mumbled out *thanks* and took a drink, the liquid burning like fire down his throat. He looked to his right and realized a pretty redhead was giving him the eye. He offered a brief smile before angling away from her. The girl was flashy, obviously on the make. He'd been around her type enough to know that he wasn't interested.

He looked to his left and did a double-take. It was her—the blonde he'd seen when he first arrived. Sitting a few seats away from him. As stunning as she'd been from afar, she was even more so up close. Her hair fell over her shoulders in a sheet of glimmering honey. The form-fitting red dress hugged her curves in a classy way. He'd hoped she might look his direction, so he could get her attention, but she was staring down at her drink, like her mind was a thousand miles away. Sure, she was beautiful, but there were lots of beautiful women in this room. For a moment, he couldn't pinpoint what it was about her that had captured his attention. Then it hit him—it was the haunted expression on her face. It called to his own wounded soul.

Corbin's throat went dry as he swallowed, his pulse ratcheting up a few notches. He had to get to know this woman. The compulsion was nearly overwhelming. He laughed inwardly. Was he losing it? He'd gotten very little sleep the night before. Maybe exhaustion was taking its toll. The woman had given him the brush-off. She obviously wasn't interested in him. He took another swallow of his drink, his blood pumping like a piston through his veins.

Before his mind could register what his body was doing, he stood, drink in hand. Without asking for permission, he sat down beside her. Her eyes widened as she glanced at him.

"Hello." A stupid grin washed over his face. He didn't really know what he expected would happen when he made the split-second decision to sit down beside a stranger and try to start up a conversation. But he certainly didn't expect her to give him such a scathing look, like he was the scum of the earth, before turning her attention back to her glass.

Hot needles pricked over him. *Shot down before you even got off the ground.* He was a big boy and could handle it. Earlier, she'd noticed him first. He'd felt her eyes on him, which is why she initially caught his attention. "Nice party."

She grunted.

He laughed. "That exciting, huh?" He downed the rest of his drink with a couple of swallows, feeling the alcohol buzz to his head. He couldn't believe she was flat-out ignoring him. Not the sort of treatment he was used to getting from the opposite sex. Normally, he had to beat the women off him. He watched as she stirred her straw through the ice cubes and took a drink. The graceful movements of her slim fingers were mesmerizing. A smile flitted over his lips as he realized what was happening. She was playing hard-to-get. He loved a good chase. It made things ... interesting.

The bartender approached. "Can I get you another drink?"

"I'll have what she's having," Corbin said casually. He thought that would at least earn him some sort of response.

Nothing.

Okay, this was getting awkward. Maybe he should cut bait and move on.

"Here you go," the bartender said, sliding the drink to him.

"I don't see it," Corbin said.

Silence.

"Are you sure it's there?"

At that, she turned. "What?" she asked, only mildly interested.

"Whatever it is you find so fascinating at the bottom of your drink."

She arched an eyebrow. "Excuse me?"

He motioned, fighting a smile. "You were staring into your glass like it held the secret of the Bermuda Triangle, so I figured it must be important." He expected her to at least give him a courtesy laugh for the effort, but she just rolled her eyes and turned her attention back to her glass.

Corbin took a gulp of the drink, then sputtered in disgust. "This is club soda."

She cut her eyes at him. "You have such discriminating taste."

At least he'd caught her attention, but her words were flat and dead. Not even the slightest bit of emotion in them. *Sheesh.* This woman was tough. "Are you always this friendly?" he asked dryly.

As she turned to face him, his mind cataloged her features. Long lashes, dark mysterious eyes, full lips painted apple red to match her dress. Her brow lifted in faint amusement. "Are you always this desperate?"

Her soft Southern accent was such a contrast to her insult that it rendered him speechless for a second. "I would hardly call trying to make polite conversation desperate."

"Is that what you call this?"

"Of course," he blustered. What was it about this woman that was making him so jumpy? He never got tongue-tied around women. Normally, the compliments rolled out of him like ballads with the ladies eating up every word. But not this woman. He forced a laugh. "Well, yeah. What else?"

She shrugged. "A poor attempt at hitting on me."

"Don't flatter yourself," he retorted. Her eyes widened in surprise before her face flushed, making her look even more incredible. He felt kind of bad for cutting her down and tried to think of a way to soften the blow. Then it occurred to him. She looked familiar. He cocked his head, trying to figure out where he'd seen her. "Have we met before? Do you live here, in San Diego?"

Her mouth drew into a tight line. "That's none of your business."

"I wasn't trying to pry ... only trying to figure out how I know you. Have you ever been to Birchwood Springs, Colorado?"

She clipped out a single word. "Nope."

Corbin was unprepared for the sting of disappointment that prickled through him. This woman meant nothing to him. Why was he taking her rejection so personally? She'd clearly dismissed him. The polite thing to do would be to get up and move. But Corbin had never been one to follow the rules of decorum. "What's your name?"

Her eyes widened in exasperation as she turned to him. "Buddy, can't you take a hint? I'm not interested."

He cocked an eyebrow. "I'm only trying to carry on a conversation."

Her jaw tightened. "I'm going to ask you one final time. Leave me alone."

"Okay, I will. But first, you have to tell me your name." *Geez.* He was coming across as a love-starved jerk. He'd come here to meet with Sutton, not pick up on chicks. But this woman was messing with his head. Crazy, because he didn't even know her. And she obviously had zero interest in him, but she'd been checking him out earlier. Talk about mixed signals! This woman was a master at it.

She looked past Corbin, exchanging some sort of information with the person behind him. Corbin turned as a heavyset guy with bulging biceps approached. His thick brows bunched as he sized-up Corbin. "Is this guy giving you problems, Miss Mitchell?" His voice had a warning edge, the kind tough-guys used in the hope it would send all opposition running. *Not gonna happen, buddy.*

The name clicked, as Corbin experienced an a-ha moment. "You're Delaney Mitchell, that country music singer." No wonder she was being standoffish. She was probably used to guys trying to pick up on her. Then he remembered hearing something about her on the news. She'd shot her ex-husband when he broke into her condo. Yep, the woman had some major baggage. He had to laugh at himself. A roomful of people, and he was drawn to the one who was as messed up as he was. Par for his luck.

"I tried to tell him I wasn't interested, but he won't take a hint," Delaney said.

"I was only trying to make conversation," Corbin mumbled. "You looked lonely ... like you needed a friend." Why was he even bothering to explain himself to this woman? Her gaze connected with his. For a split second, something flickered in Delaney's eyes and he caught that wounded expression that had drawn him in. Then a curtain went down, her eyes going hard. "I told you to leave me alone," she said coldly.

Without thinking, he touched her arm. "Hey," he began.

It was the wrong move. The big man grabbed Corbin's collar and yanked him to his feet. "Come with me," he ordered.

Instinct took over as Corbin threw a punch that connected with the man's jaw. He heard the crack at the same instant the sting of the impact reverberated through his knuckles. The big man stumbled back, disoriented. Corbin side-swept his leg, sending him crashing to the ground. There were several gasps from people nearby as they stepped back. Their shocked faces cut through the heady anger, making Corbin feel ashamed. He'd come here to honor his late friend and to reconnect with Sutton, not get in a bar brawl with some hoity toity musician's bodyguard.

He gave Delaney a disgusted look. "I was only trying to get to know you. Lady, you have much too high of an opinion of yourself." He grunted. "Good riddance." He bent over to offer the guy a hand up. The guy clutched his hand, but instead of using it to get up. He pulled Corbin forward and punched him in the jaw. Pain rippled through Corbin and with that pain came a scorching anger that overshadowed reason. They rolled on the floor, trading blows. Then Corbin sprang to his feet, adrenaline coursing through his veins. He could go like this all night. In some perverse way, it felt good to vent the anger and frustration continually warring inside him. The man also lumbered to his feet. He wiped the thin trail of blood flowing from his lip, breathing heavily. A humorless grin ruffled Corbin's lips. "Have you had enough? You should've left well enough alone, friend. I was trying to help you up."

The hulk lunged at him, but Corbin easily dodged out of his way. A crowd had circled around them. It just went to show that regardless of whether folks were high or low-class, they loved the thrill of the fight.

The man came at him again. Corbin stepped to the side causing the lug to run headfirst into the bar. Corbin assumed that would be the end of it, but the hulk turned to face him, his eyes dark slashes as he shook off the hit. When he charged again, Corbin twisted behind him and got him in a chokehold. The man's face turned purple, his arms flailing. Then he slumped to his knees and fell face-first on the floor, passed out cold.

Corbin glanced down at the streaks of blood on his white tux jacket. He looked at Delaney, who was ghostly white. "It didn't have to be this way." He rubbed his jaw, still smarting from the hits, then glanced at the spectators. "Show's over," he grumbled.

He got a couple of steps away when four security guards in black suits approached. He crouched getting into a fighting position. So this is how they wanted to play it. Fine with him! When the first guy charged, he clocked him in the face, knocking him down. He got the second with a swift sidekick to the gut. As he was fighting the third, the fourth attacked from behind. A sharp pain splintered up the base of his skull as he fell to his knees, the room spinning. His mind screamed *fight*, but his body refused to cooperate. In another second, the security guards had Corbin pinned on the ground, slapping handcuffs on his wrists. They lifted him to his feet, breathing curses as they hauled him away.

4

From what Corbin could tell, he'd been placed in a holding cell in some deep underground section of the mansion. The walls were solid metal with the door being the only opening. Corbin had yelled for several minutes, demanding to be released, but the box was as soundproof as a tomb. Finally, he slumped down in the metal chair beside the table. Two chairs and a table were the only furniture in the room.

It was crazy how fast things had escalated out of control. One minute, he was attempting to talk to Delaney. And the next, he was fighting with the big guy, whom he assumed was Delaney's bodyguard. The anger had taken over, the way it had been doing for some time now. But Corbin hadn't started this fight. Trouble seemed to follow him wherever he went. He rumbled out a sarcastic laugh. Was this Sutton Smith's plan all along? Lure him here so he could keep him prisoner?

No, there was no reason for Sutton to have a grudge against Corbin. If anything, Sutton should be glad that Corbin had tried to avenge Doug's death the day of the ambush. Of course, everything went terribly wrong. But that was beside the point. Corbin, more than anyone except Sutton, had felt the agony of Doug's death. And with that pain came the guilt of what happened afterward.

The door opened, and Sutton stepped through. He strode over and sat down in the chair on the opposite side of the table. Even though Sutton was dressed impeccably in an expensive tux, he was all grit and muscle, his movements as nimble as a panther. The type of guy you didn't want to cross. His blue eyes flickered over Corbin. "I'm glad to see the tux was sent to you as instructed." After decades in the US, Sutton still had a slight British accent.

Corbin glanced down at the stains. "I hope you included dry cleaning in the package." He noticed that Sutton had left the door open. Maybe that was a good sign that he'd let Corbin out of here soon.

A slight smile touched Sutton's lips in acknowledgement of Corbin's poor attempt at humor, then vanished almost as quickly as it had come. "It's been a while. How've you been?"

Seriously? The guy wanted to make conversation. "I'd be a lot better if I weren't handcuffed." He gave Sutton a hard look. "Why're you keeping me here?"

"I had hoped to have this conversation on friendlier terms. But I didn't expect you to get into a fight the minute you stepped in the door." His voice held a note of irony.

Corbin's jaw tightened. "I didn't start it. It was that meathead bodyguard—"

Amusement flickered in Sutton's eyes. "I know what happened. I saw the security feed." His eyebrows shot up, wrinkling his forehead. "You handled yourself pretty well." He shrugged. "At least until the end, when you were put down."

He didn't appreciate the assessment, nor the jab. "Four on one's hardly fair." It was no surprise that Sutton had cameras everywhere. This conversation was probably being recorded right now. He glanced around, seeing no evidence of a camera. But that didn't mean one wasn't hidden somewhere.

Sutton chuckled. "I'd think by now you would've learned that life is anything but fair."

Somehow Corbin knew Sutton was talking about Doug. It got him like a punch in the gut. He caught a blip of Sutton's hurt mirroring his own. He swallowed the ball in his throat. He looked Sutton in the eye. "Why did you pay for me to come here?"

"I have a proposition for you."

"Something other than being handcuffed and thrown in a cell?" He shot Sutton an accusing look.

"You brought that on yourself, lad."

Corbin was getting fed up with dancing around the topic. "What do you want from me?"

"I'm holding a meeting." He glanced at his watch. "It starts in five minutes. I'd like for you to attend, and I'll explain everything."

He pinned Sutton with a look. "You'll tell me now. I'm tired of playing games. I wore the tux, came to your stupid party, got mauled by your security guards, and thrown into some holding cell. Enough is enough."

Sutton quirked a half smile. "You have a couple of options here."

"I'm listening."

"In a couple of minutes, someone's going to come in and remove your handcuffs." He reached in his jacket and retrieved an envelope. "Here's the money you were promised." He placed it on the table. "You can take it and go your merry way, or you can stick around for the meeting—hear about a unique opportunity that could be yours, if you have enough sense to recognize it."

"I don't need anything from you," Corbin growled. "I'm doing just fine on my own."

"Obviously, with your bar bouncer job and part-time security gig at the movie theater."

Corbin flinched. "You've had me checked out." He didn't need to have it pointed out that he'd reached a low point in his life. "Why?"

Sutton let out a long sigh. "Look, I know what happened right after Doug died."

The words came at Corbin like a sledgehammer as he gasped, shame burning over him. "H—how?" he sputtered. Those records were sealed. Then again there were probably very few things in this world a man like Sutton Smith couldn't access.

A fierce light came into Sutton's eyes as he continued. "I know the anger that fuels you. I've felt it myself." He paused. "In fact, it almost destroyed me," he said softly. He clutched his fist. "Here's the bottom line, I'm offering you a chance to do something meaningful with your life. And I'll pay you handsomely in the process."

"Why do you give a crap about me?" Corbin rattled off reflexively.

Sutton straightened his shoulders, not taking his eyes off Corbin's. "Because my son gave a crap about you, that's why."

Moisture rose in Corbin's eyes as he blinked. "Doug was the best friend I ever had." He coughed to hide his emotion, looking down at the table.

"He loved you like a brother. For what's it's worth, thank you."

Corbin's head shot up. "For what?"

"For caring enough about Doug to come here tonight. And for keeping my son's memory alive."

The gravity of Sutton's words hit Corbin full force. Something swift and strong flowed between them. They would always be connected through Doug's life and then later his death.

A man stepped in. Corbin recognized him as one of the security guards who'd tackled him earlier. The guy shot Corbin a surly look. It gave him a ping of satisfaction when he saw the guy's swollen lip. He stepped behind Corbin and removed the handcuffs. Then he turned on his heel and left the room in a hurry like he feared a rematch. Corbin stood, glancing at the envelope and then at Sutton.

Sutton rose to his feet. "What will it be?"

He tugged at his jacket. "I'm in no hurry. I'll go to the meeting."

Sutton looked pleased. "Very well." He motioned. "This way."

"WHAT IS THIS?" Corbin glared at the four faces seated around the conference room table. Blayze, River, Zane, and Cannon ... fellow members of SEAL Team 7—four people he hoped to never lay eyes on again. They looked just as surprised to see him.

Sutton motioned. "Have a seat."

Blood thrashed against Corbin's temples as his feet stayed rooted to the floor, his fists clutching into balls. "Whatever this is, I don't want any part of it." He couldn't believe Sutton had dragged him here to face these guys. *So much for opportunity.*

River smirked at Zane, who was sitting beside him. "No surprise there."

Corbin's body tensed. "What do you mean by that?" He was ready to pound some heads.

Zane AKA Thor because of his striking resemblance to the Marvel hero, made a point of eyeing the blood streaks on his jacket. "Same old Corbin, huh? Always got somebody's blood on your hands."

The comment was the match that lit the wildfire. He pounced at Zane who sprang to his feet. Corbin managed to strike a fist to Zane's cheekbone before Zane landed a punch of his own that knocked Corbin back against the table. It was one thing to spar with a lumbering bodyguard, but another to fight a fellow Navy SEAL who was Corbin's equal in every way. Still, there was no backing down from this. Corbin got back up, ready to go again. He swung, but Zane ducked. Corbin took another shot. Zane stepped out of the way, but Corbin ran at him, the two toppling to the floor.

The other guys pulled them apart.

"Enough, already!" Cannon yelled, stepping between them. A volunteer, lay pastor, Cannon was normally the easy-going one in the group, determined to help keep the peace. It was always an uphill task considering they were a group of alpha males, constantly vying to be top-dog.

Zane's brow shot up, a derisive chuckle barking out of his lips. "Careful, Cannon. You know how Corbin hates taking orders from superiors."

The comment was a knife in the gut. Zane had been the commanding officer in their platoon. He took it as a personal insult when Corbin defied his order on the day Doug was killed. And he'd never let Corbin forget it. "Respect has to be earned, not demanded." It was probably not the best comeback, but the only one Corbin could come up with.

Zane shook his head in disgust. "Exactly. And you lost our respect the day you hung us out to dry."

Sutton held up his hands. "Gentlemen, if you'll please take your seats." He looked at Corbin. "And put a lid on your anger for a few minutes, you might find this conversation beneficial."

All eyes turned to Corbin, waiting for his reaction.

"I'm not sure it's possible for him to cork his anger," Zane said, an open challenge simmering in his eyes. "Why don't you just tap the brass bell right now and save us all the trouble?"

It was a low blow, referring to the brass bell which sat in the courtyard at BUD/S Training. When guys couldn't hack the drills they'd ring the bell three times, signaling that they'd had enough, at which point they'd forfeit their chance to become a SEAL and receive another Naval assignment. Before Zane's comment, Corbin was ready to leave this room, turn his back on these men forever. But now, the only way anyone would drag him out of here would be in a body bag.

He lifted his chin and sat down in the closest seat, crossing his arms over his chest, his jaw set in stone. He could feel the other guys watching him. There was a time when he'd loved these guys like brothers, almost as much as he'd loved Doug. Their team had a reputation for being one of the best. That all changed the night Doug got killed. Deep down, Corbin didn't blame the guys for hating him. He hated himself for what happened. All the training in the world, his former achievements, none of it would be enough to make up for those few short, dreadful minutes when he'd lost it and gone on the rampage.

Sutton cleared his throat. "You're wondering why I asked you to come here tonight."

"The thought has crossed our minds."

This came from Blayze who was sitting on the opposite side of the table. Expert at reading people and situations, Corbin could tell from the intense look on Blayze's face that he was trying to get a read on Sutton. Corbin risked a glance at Cannon who gave him a slight smile. For an instant, Corbin was taken off guard by the kindness. Then again, Cannon had always preached the value of turning the other cheek. Corbin offered a quick nod of acknowledgement before turning his attention back to Sutton.

"All of you are highly trained, retired SEALs. Men who can be trusted. Men whom my son Doug trusted."

Corbin's skin crawled a little at that. He knew none of the men in this room trusted him any further than they could throw him. They felt like he'd broken the code and betrayed their trust. Well, maybe he had, but he'd certainly not done it intentionally. If he could relive that day and react differently to Doug's death, he would in a heartbeat.

Furthermore, everyone around this table would be a little squir-relly at the mention of *Doug's trust*. None of them knew for sure whether it had been enemy or friendly fire that killed Doug. Had Sutton brought them here to exact revenge? A shiver raced down Corbin's spine. Maybe the billionaire philanthropist wasn't so benevolent, after all. He pushed aside the misgiving. He and Sutton had shared a moment in the holding cell—he saw it in Sutton's eyes, felt it rattle his core. He and Sutton shared a bond. They'd both loved Doug, both had been completely devastated by Doug's death. Sutton said this was an opportunity, and Corbin believed the man was being truthful.

"In case you're wondering, I know every last detail surrounding Doug's death," Sutton continued, stroking his short beard, which was more pepper than salt.

An uncomfortable silence froze over the group. The only reason the five former SEALs were alive was because Doug had chosen to die so they could escape the ambush.

Sutton looked around the room, his intense gaze meeting every eye. "I don't hold any of you responsible. It was a tragic accident." His voice quivered so slightly that Corbin wondered if he'd only imagined it. "The one consolation is knowing Doug died serving his country and fellow SEALs."

Corbin remembered Doug mentioning that Sutton was a Commodore in the Royal Navy. He would have a personal appreciation and respect for service to country and fellow comrades.

"Doug was a cut above the rest, the embodiment of excellence," Zane said.

"Yes, he was. He never gave up on any of us." *Even when we gave up on ourselves,* Corbin added mentally. It wasn't until he saw the surprised looks that he realized he'd spoken out loud. He and Zane locked gazes and in his former commander's eyes, he caught a glimpse of mutual understanding. At least that was one point on which he and Zane could agree. Doug was the best, the glue that held the team together.

"I'm assembling a special ops group of retired Navy SEALs. Our intent will be to help those whose problems fall outside the realm of traditional law enforcement. People who are backed in a corner with nowhere else to go for help."

Zane grunted. "I think I speak for most of the guys here that under the circumstance ..." he cleared his throat cutting his eyes at Corbin "... we don't feel comfortable putting our lives in the hands of someone who's so unpredictable."

Heat burned over Corbin as his eyes narrowed. He was about to go on the rampage again, then saw the mixture of resentment and pity in Zane's eyes. It hit him in that moment, had he been in Zane's shoes, he'd probably say the same thing.

Sutton held up a hand. "Group is a loose term. You'll work as independent contractors and will be paid per assignment. Additionally, each of you will receive a souped-up, black SUV with bulletproof windows. I have other security personnel that you can have access to, should you need their assistance. Other retired SEALs will be brought in as time goes on."

Still smarting from the insults, Corbin's mind raced in circles like a hamster in a ball. No clear destination in sight, but he had to keep running all the same. It wasn't until Sutton got to the substantial sums of money they'd earn that he felt a quiver of excitement. This could be the start of a new career. The chance to do something useful. Also, it would be nice to earn some real money. Maybe get a new bike ... take a trip somewhere warm. He was tired of the Colorado snow and sick of pinching pennies.

"How will you determine which assignments we're given?" Zane asked. "Will it be done on an 'as needed' basis?"

"Good question. The jobs will be assigned according to your skill set." Sutton punched the table with his finger. "You have my word that I'll make sure you have every available resource you need to be successful." He motioned. "And while it doesn't look like it, this mansion is a veritable fortress ... a hub, from which we'll conduct our business."

Corbin's eyes popped slightly thinking about the holding cell where he'd been detained. It had been solid as a tomb. There was no telling how many secret tunnels and areas ran through the mansion.

Sutton's voice grew intense, his penetrating blue eyes scoping the room. "Gentlemen, in a small way, we'll be paying homage to Doug, helping right some of the many wrongs in this tragic world." He squared his jaw, straightening to his full height. "Let's do this. The Warrior Project. Not only for Doug, but also for God and Country."

Corbin's chest burned with a new determination. He'd come into this room floundering, no real direction in his life. But now he had something he could sink his teeth into. An unexpected feeling of hope kindled in his chest. This could be a way to get the one thing he craved most ... redemption. "The Warrior Project. For Doug, God and Country," he repeated softly.

5

When the fight broke out between Delaney's bodyguard and that annoying guy, Delaney feared Sutton might order her to leave. Thankfully, that didn't happen. After the guy was hauled away by security guards, things settled back down. Delaney cooled her heels for three more hours, waiting for the party to wind down, before Agatha found her and announced that Sutton would see her in his study.

Delaney had been a nervous wreck, not sure what to expect, but the meeting with Sutton Smith went much better than she expected. All in all, it was anticlimactic. She'd been prepared to plead her case, trying to figure out the best way to convey how truly cutthroat Hugh Allen was. As it turned out, anything she could've said would've been a waste of breath because Sutton already knew. He'd done his research on the Allens, probably knew more about their nefarious business dealings than she did. Rumors had been floating around Noble for years. Some had Hugh being an arms dealer to terrorist groups. Others said Hugh was the head of a private militia. Whatever Hugh was involved in, it wasn't good. People who crossed him disappeared. Delaney's philosophy had always been the less she knew the better.

After about ten minutes into the conversation, Delaney realized that as far as Sutton was concerned taking her on as a client was a done deal. She got the feeling he'd already made the decision even before she came here tonight. They discussed the particulars, starting with Sutton's fee, which was nominal considering the circumstance. Sutton told her he was assigning one of his top guys to provide around-the-clock protection, a retired Navy SEAL.

Considering how easily Tuck had breezed past her bodyguard, Delaney was leery of putting her fate in the hands of one individual. But Sutton assured her that the guy was well-trained, and could be as vicious as Hugh if the situation warranted.

"As cliché as it sounds, the only way to fight fire is with fire," Sutton said in a British accent. "Rest assured that your bodyguard has access to a team of people and additional resources if need be." He gave her a piercing look. "It's not looking good for your ex-husband. The doctors don't expect him to live past a few more days."

Her heart lurched as she nodded, tears springing to her eyes. "I know," she said quietly.

"You're in good hands," Sutton assured her.

A feeling of gratitude washed over Delaney. She was so appreciative of Milo who'd put her in touch with Sutton. For the first time since the ordeal with Tuck, she felt like she might have a fighting chance for survival.

Sutton stood, telling her to wait while he went to get her bodyguard. When he got to the door, he turned. "Oh, one more thing," he said casually.

She tensed slightly. "Yes?"

"In order for this to work, I need you to have complete trust in me and your bodyguard. You have to listen to his instructions, trust that he'll do everything in his power to keep you safe."

"Okay." Odd advice. Why would she do any different? She was hiring Sutton and this guy to keep her safe.

"Hang tight. I'll return shortly."

"Sounds good." She hugged her arms, glancing around at the handsome study. Bookcases lined one of the walls from floor to ceiling. Her gaze ran over the book spines. Most of the books had to do with the military, strategy, or combat. An enormous mahogany desk sat in front of the opposite wall. Underneath it was an ornate Oriental rug. The cozy space exuded old money and prestige. She scooted back into the comfort of the overstuffed chair and crossed her legs. She glanced at the large clock on the wall beside the bookshelves. She assumed that Sutton would return momentarily, but ten minutes went by, then twenty. She rested her head against the back of the chair, letting her mind get lost in the steady rhythm of the ticking clock.

Delaney stifled a yawn. Until she'd sat down, she'd not realized how tired she was from all the stress. Her eyelids grew heavy as she dozed off.

The door opened and she jumped guiltily. She sat up quickly then realized she'd been drooling. Heat crept up her neck as she wiped it away.

"Sorry that took so long," Sutton said.

"No worries," she said automatically, then her eyes popped when she realized who was standing behind him. "You!" Her mind reeled. "I thought the security guards took you away."

"Sorry, darling, I'm not that easy to get rid of," he said dryly. He held out his hand, an expression of faint amusement on his handsome face. "Corbin Spencer. Nice to officially meet you."

She just looked at his extended hand like it was a snake about to strike. This couldn't be happening! He chuckled and dropped his hand to his side. A blistering heat slapped Delaney's cheeks as she gripped the arms of the chair. Was this some sort of cruel joke? Surely this guy wasn't her bodyguard. An incredulous laugh bubbled in her throat as she looked at Sutton. "Are you kidding me?"

Sutton's expression never changed as his eyes met hers. "You and I agreed that you would trust me to pair you with the best man for the job. I've done that."

"No, I don't want him." She shook her head back and forth. "There must be someone else." The thought of this guy being around her twenty-four-seven was too much to take. Even now attraction was zinging through her veins despite her best effort to squelch it. She couldn't get involved with someone right now, especially not this guy. He was a hothead, all fire and excitement that would burn her to the core, leaving only ashes. She squared her jaw, glaring at Corbin.

Sutton flashed a friendly smile. "You came here for my help, right?"

"Yes," she said hesitantly.

"Then let me help you." His eyes locked with hers. "Corbin's the best guy for the job. You have to trust me on this."

Trust. A double-edged sword. The hard set of Sutton's jaw let her know that he wasn't backing down. She ran a hand through her hair. Moisture rose in her eyes as the walls closed in around her. She blinked a few times, trying to clear the emotion. It was ridiculous to get so worked up about this. She had to have help. It was a miracle that she'd even found Sutton. No one else she was aware of could stand up against Hugh. "Okay," she finally said, exhaling a long breath.

Sutton nodded. "Very good. Corbin has been briefed on the situation. He'll leave here with you and move into your condo immediately. It's imperative that you not spend a minute alone until the threat is contained or eliminated."

Alarm trickled down her spine. She didn't know which she feared most—Hugh or having Corbin so close. "What about your things ... luggage?" Had Corbin come to the party because he was going to be assigned to help her? Another thought struck, making her feel like a complete idiot. Maybe Corbin approached her at the bar to tell her he'd be guarding her. And she assumed he was trying to hit on her. *Sheesh*. This was getting way too complicated.

Sutton turned to Corbin. "I'll have someone go to the hotel and retrieve your bags."

"Thank you." Corbin said with a slight nod.

Hotel? Why was Corbin staying in a hotel? Did he not live in San Diego? Now that she thought about it, she shouldn't have been all that surprised that Corbin was a former Navy SEAL. She'd known he was tough from the moment she saw him. At least he was on the good team ... or so it appeared. At this point, she didn't trust anyone. Tuck was good at feigning kindness to get what he wanted. He'd used her love for him as a weapon against her. And now, even his impending death was a threat to her. There seemed to be no end to the treachery.

"It's probably wise to take the bullet-proof SUV instead of the rental car," Sutton added.

Bullet-proof? Delaney's stomach churned thinking about the gravity of the situation. Tuck could die any minute, and she'd have a target on her back. Heck, who was she kidding? She was already a target. For all she knew, Hugh was waiting right outside to ambush her. She hugged her arms, sloughing off the shiver that crawled down her spine.

Sutton brought his hands together. "That's all for now." His voice went brisk as he looked at Corbin. "Call me anytime, day or night, on the secure line."

"Will do. You can count on me," Corbin said. And from the tone of his voice, Delaney could tell he meant it. That made her feel a little better about things.

She stood. "Thank you. I appreciate all that you're doing." She didn't want Sutton to think she was an ungrateful brat because of her outburst over Corbin. Sutton was a gift sent straight from heaven. She hoped with all her heart that Corbin would be able to keep her safe. She thought of something else. "Will I be able to go about my normal routine?" The deadline for the album was looming over her. The execs at Montana Crew Label were being very understanding about her situation, but she didn't want to do anything to mess up her big shot.

"We certainly hope that's the case," Sutton answered. "There are no guarantees. We'll just have to see how this thing plays out."

She nodded, her lips forming a grim line. "I understand." She appreciated Sutton's honesty and that he wasn't just paying her lip service.

A brief smile touched Sutton's lips as he looked from Delaney to Corbin. "I'll leave you to it. Good luck."

When he left the room, Delaney was keenly aware that she and

Corbin were alone. An awkward silence descended between them. Should she apologize for earlier? Or just leave well enough alone?

"Are you ready?"

"Huh?" It was hard to form a clear thought with Corbin so close. Plus, she was exhausted. She hoped her mind would turn off tonight so she could get some sleep. Oh, how she desperately needed it.

"To go to your condo."

"Oh, yeah." He probably thought she was a complete moron. Where else would they go? Sutton mentioned that Corbin had been briefed about her situation. How much did Sutton know about her relationship with Tuck? Did he realize that Tuck had abused her for so many years? It was embarrassing that she'd been weak enough to let it happen. She tried to keep a lid on her past as much as she could. But now that she'd shot Tuck and put him in the hospital everything was splitting wide open.

"You ready?" A hint of amusement flickered in his green eyes. Or were they gold? Whatever color they were, they were mesmerizing. She took in his features—messy, nut-brown hair, olive skin, prominent cheekbones, white even teeth, razor-sharp jaw that had a stubborn set. A heatwave blasted over her when she realized that he'd caught her staring at him. This was the second time tonight.

She lifted her chin and forced her feet to move forward. "Yes. Where is the SUV parked?"

"In the back."

"All right. Lead the way." She wondered how long it would take before this incredible attraction subsided. Hopefully, it would be soon, or else she'd make a complete fool out of herself.

6

It was crazy how drastically Corbin's life had changed in a matter of a few hours. When he realized who his first assignment was, Corbin was shocked beyond words. Interesting that in a crowded room, he'd been drawn to Delaney. Of course, she'd noticed him first. Then she acted so cold at the bar. He wished they'd not met each other the way they had. It was making everything awkward.

They drove in silence to Delaney's condo. All the while, Corbin's brain raced to come up with witty comments, but he couldn't seem to make his tongue speak the words. When they arrived, Corbin shifted his focus from this tension with Delaney to the logistics of how to keep her safe. He couldn't let her mess with his mind and keep him from doing his job.

From what he could tell, her high-rise building had top-notch security ... a doorman, guard at the front desk, cameras, and most likely a few guards manning the parking garage. Plus, Delaney had hired a service that provided bodyguard protection around the clock. In fact, the same guy who'd fought with Corbin at the bar followed them back to Delaney's apartment. The big man's jaw had dropped to the floor when he realized the very guy he'd had an altercation with would be Delaney's primary protection detail.

All in all, Anton seemed like a decent guy. Now that Corbin understood the situation, he could see why Anton acted the way he did. Anton held up his hands in a gesture of truce. "Hey man, I had no idea who you were. Sorry about what happened earlier. I just saw someone harassing Miss Mitchell and reacted." His eyes widened. "I mean, I saw what I thought was harassment," he corrected, his face going red.

Corbin could tell Anton was sincere. Also, the poor guy looked haggard with a ripped shirt, black eye and swollen lip; whereas Corbin's jaw was a little sore and the tux stained, but that was it. One of those situations where, *If you think I look bad, you should see the other guy* applied.

"We're cool," he'd told Anton, and he meant it. Corbin couldn't blame the guy for doing his job. And it couldn't hurt to have someone parked outside Delaney's door. Of course, Tuck Allen had blown right past the high-rise security and bodyguard. Corbin had no doubt that Hugh could also break past security and get to Delaney if he so desired. His jaw hardened. What Hugh wouldn't be counting on, however, was him.

During his briefing session, Sutton had shown Corbin video footage of the night Tuck broke into Delaney's condo. He and his female accomplice slipped through the back during a furniture delivery. Then the woman changed into a revealing dress and pretended to be a tipsy party-goer who'd gotten locked out of her room, a few doors down from Delaney's. She flirted with the bodyguard and offered him the doughnuts pumped with a strong sedative. When the gullible man was passed out cold, Tuck used his key to enter the apartment.

Tuck's plan had been relatively simple, yet spot-on effective. Sutton promised to keep Corbin informed about Tuck's condition, as the threat seemingly hinged on that. Corbin didn't like being put in a vulnerable position, waiting for Hugh to attack. He asked Sutton why they didn't attack Hugh first. But Sutton explained that Hugh Allen was elusive with many protective layers around him. "It's better to let him come to you, then cut off the head of the snake. Otherwise, there would be too much risk and collateral damage."

"You can sleep here." Delaney opened the door to the guest room which was a couple doors down from the master bedroom. "Sorry about the mess." She went to the bed and grabbed an armful of clothes. "I use this room as storage," she explained. "I'll just put these in my bedroom."

"Okay, thanks." The room was nice—much cleaner than his bedroom on a good day. Delaney's high-rise condo was classy, the large windows offering a spectacular view of the city. Unfortunately, that wouldn't work for the situation. The first thing Corbin made Delaney do when they got inside the condo was close the blinds. Even though she was high up, there were other buildings close enough for someone with a high-powered telescope to have a bird's-eye view.

Delaney came back into the room. Her pinched expression said it all. She was uneasy around him. Now that Corbin realized what had happened with her ex-husband, he understood why she'd given him the brush-off earlier. He felt a little guilty for pressing her. It was probably good that she wasn't interested in him. They needed to keep this professional. More than anything, Corbin wanted to prove to Sutton that he could keep Delaney safe at all costs. To do that, he couldn't let himself get distracted by the vulnerable look on Delaney's delicate, heart-shaped face or the gentle sway of her hips as she glided in her sleek heels. The way her glorious hair bounced on her shoulders. He coughed, wondering if he should clear the air tonight or wait until the morning.

"I'm sorry you don't have any of your things." Her voice trailed off.

He could wing it tonight, no big deal.

She pointed at the adjoining bathroom. "You'll find a toothpaste and toothbrush in the top, right-hand drawer of the vanity."

"Thanks." He shoved his hands in his pockets and rocked forward on the balls of his feet.

"Well, I think I'll turn in for the night. Do you need anything?"

"I think I'm good. I plan to do a check of the condo, make sure everything's secure before I turn in for the night." The relief that came over her face shot a pang through his heart. Sutton didn't go into the details about Delaney's former marriage, but if her ex-husband were anything like his brother, it must've been a harrowing experience. He wondered how a girl like Delaney could've gotten mixed up with Tuck Allen. Then again, everyone always said love was blind. He was itching to know how Delaney felt about Tuck being in the hospital. She'd shot her former husband, someone she once loved. That had to bite. There were so many questions he wanted to ask her ... about her past, her climb to stardom, her hobbies, what she liked to eat. He laughed inwardly. Okay, he needed to take it down a notch. This was business, not a date.

She was to the door, about to step out of the room when he spoke. "Delaney?"

She turned. "Yes?"

"I'm sorry about what happened earlier ... at the bar."

Her jaw went slack as she fast-blinked a couple of times.

"If I'd realized the situation, I wouldn't have been so forward."

A polite smile fixed over her face. "Thanks."

He could almost see the wall going up between them. She was determined to keep him at a distance. Disappointment settled heavily in his gut.

"I had no idea who you were, or I wouldn't have been so cold." Pink tinged her cheeks. "I thought you were trying to hit on me."

A laugh rumbled in his throat. Should he tell her the truth? Or should he keep that to himself? He winked. "And here I thought that you were hitting on me, when you checked me out as I came into the party." He relished the deep blush that colored her cheeks. She was gorgeous. He had the unreasonable urge to pull her into his arms and see if her lips tasted as good as they looked.

Her eyes narrowed as she straightened her shoulders. "I was not checking you out."

Even though her voice was edged with outrage, Corbin couldn't get over how lyrical her accent was—as smooth as Gram's lemon chiffon pie with just the right amount of huskiness. A smile tugged at his lips. It was fun teasing her. "I guess we'll have to agree to disagree."

She lifted her chin, her eyes sparkling. "You can be a real jerk sometimes."

The insult took him off guard as he laughed. Sparring with Delaney was much better than the awkward silence. He winked. "Only fifty percent of the time."

Her hand went to her hip, but he could tell she was trying not to smile. "Oh? And what about the other fifty percent?"

"Charming ... witty ... a perfect gentleman."

She grunted. "I doubt that."

"It's true," he said with a straight face.

"You're humble too," she said sarcastically.

He took a step closer to her, his pulse pumping up a notch. "So, Delaney Mitchell ... are you gonna sing me a bedtime song if I can't get to sleep?" He cringed inwardly. Not the most appropriate comment, but he couldn't seem to reel himself in around Delaney. He really liked her, wanted to get to know her.

She blushed again, her chocolate-colored eyes popping indignantly. "You wish."

He laughed. "Can't blame a guy for trying." He made a mental note to use his phone to Google Delaney before he went to sleep. He wanted to know more about her career. Mostly, he wanted to hear how her sultry voice would sound when put to music.

"I think I'll leave on that note," she clipped. "You know where the kitchen is. Help yourself to whatever you need. I've got to leave for the recording studio at eight a.m. We'll eat a quick breakfast and head out."

"Sounds good." His gaze locked with hers, and he felt again that same connection he'd experienced when he first arrived at the party. He could tell from the look in Delaney's eyes that she was attracted to him too. But she was also scared of her feelings. It was crazy how he could be so in tune with a woman he'd only just met. But he felt her thoughts as if they were his own. Anger pulsed through his veins. It was probably a good thing Tuck Allen was in a coma. Otherwise, Corbin would've been tempted to beat the man to a pulp for hurting Delaney.

Suddenly, he wished he were sleeping in the same room with Delaney. Not necessarily because he was so attracted to her, but because he wanted to keep a close eye on her in case Hugh Allen tried anything. His mind did a risk assessment. It would be nearly impossible for Hugh to enter from the patio. He'd have to come through the door like Tuck had done. Or try to get to Delaney in transit or at the studio.

He sat down on the edge of the bed and removed his shoes. His shoulder blades were tight with tension. "What else do you have planned for tomorrow other than a trip to your recording studio?" If he knew the agenda, he could get prepared for any surprises. He loosened the bowtie and removed the tux jacket. He wasn't sure what time in the morning Sutton's guy was bringing his luggage, but it had better be early. He didn't want to wear this getup any longer than he had to. He made a mental note to text Sutton before he went to bed.

"Tomorrow night, I'm singing at Senator Fleming's birthday party."

He winced. "What? Sutton didn't mention anything about that."

"Well, probably because he didn't know," Delaney retorted. "I met Sutton for the first time, shortly before he brought you into the study."

Corbin was surprised by that. Then again, he shouldn't have been. From what he could tell, Sutton tended to act swiftly with very little explanation. It would be a challenge to protect Delaney in a large group, especially when she was performing. He'd have to ask Sutton to send over a team of bodyguards. He rubbed a hand over his jaw. This was getting more complicated by the minute. Then again, you didn't get paid the kind of money he was getting for easy. The SEAL motto flitted through his mind. *The only easy day was yesterday.*

Delaney leaned against the doorframe, her hands going into the air. "I can't just put my life on hold because of this threat. I have commitments ... obligations. My career is just now taking off. To stop now would be career suicide." Delaney's forehead creased, her eyes heavy with exhaustion, shoulders sagging. She removed her stilettos, holding them both in one hand.

"I understand where you're coming from, but to knowingly put yourself in a risky situation could also be suicide ... literally."

Her face paled, making her look vulnerable and lost. He was taken back by the fierce protectiveness that welled in his chest. Again, he wanted to gather her in his arms, soothe the worry lines from her beautiful face. She gave him a pleading look. "What other choice do I have? I have to sing tomorrow night."

It only took him a second to reach a decision. He'd never been able to stand by idly when there was a woman in need. Of course, he'd lost count of the number of times that philosophy had gotten him in fights, many of which landed him in jail. But that was beside the point. "Okay, we'll go with it. Tomorrow morning, before we head out, we need to sit down and go over your schedule. That way, I'll know what's coming."

"Agreed."

He pressed his fingers into his eye sockets, then rubbed them over his forehead, and back through his hair. He needed a good night's sleep so he could look at the situation through fresh eyes. Because right now, all he could think was that he was alone in a condo with the most intoxicating woman he'd ever met. He was supposed to keep her safe from a very dangerous and immediate threat. And all he could think about was kissing her until neither of them could think straight. He realized she was studying him, an enigmatic expression on her face. "What?"

A slight smile touched her lips. "I know we didn't get off to the greatest start, but thanks for being here." She hesitated. "It's nice to know someone has my back ..." she shuddered, her voice losing sound, "in case."

This was serious ... the threat large ... Delaney's life on the line. He had to remain sharp, push aside the attraction he felt for her. Something as indefinable as a whisper yet stronger than steel wafted over him as his eyes met Delaney's. This thing between them was real

... more than physical. He felt her pain, knew in some indescribable way that even though they'd only just met, he'd go to the end of the earth and back for this woman if necessary. "You need to know that I'll do everything in my power to keep you safe ... whatever it takes."

Her eyes teared up. "Somehow, I know that," she uttered, then looked surprised that she'd said it. "Good night," she quipped, then quickly left the room.

"Good night," Corbin repeated softly. He was starting to recognize a pattern. Every time something sparked between them, Delaney retreated. It's probably for the best, his mind argued, even though his heart didn't believe it.

SHE WAS STANDING in a field of clover, the one where she used to play as a child ... wiling away many a lazy summer afternoon making long flower chains that she'd wind around her head as a crown. A chill ran over her flesh as she looked around, noticing that the world had gone dark. She looked up, trying to see the sun, but an ominous cloud was in the way. Delaney ran full speed, trying to escape the shadow of the cloud, but no matter where she went, the cloud seemed to follow.

She looked in the distance and saw him coming toward her. Her first thought was to get away, but she was transfixed by the splendor of this man. Tall with lean sinewy muscles, he walked with purpose, a warrior strength in his jaw. Before she realized, he was standing in front of her.

"I shouldn't be here. I can't be attracted to you." She pointed up at the cloud, fright knotting her insides. "I have to get away."

Corbin only smiled in amusement, sending her pulse racing. She stared into his mesmerizing eyes ... greener than a grove of trees with specks of gold. In the tenderness of his gaze, she caught the faint notes of a ballad that only her heart could understand. Her defenses crumbled like a broken suit of armor at her feet.

Her stomach tingled as his arm encircled her waist and pulled her to him in a crushing embrace. "I can't," she uttered before his lips came down on hers. Gently his lips moved against hers, stoking the growing fire until it became an inferno of splendid emotion. Her hands moved across his back and up through his hair as she pulled him closer. Never had she felt such utter and complete bliss as she drank in his nearness.

The scene shifted. It wasn't Corbin but Tuck who held her in his arms. His blue eyes were balls of ice, his mouth twisted in a cruel smile as he squeezed her to the point where she couldn't breathe. As her eyes bulged, he laughed. His mocking laughter grew louder and more terrible until it shook the very ground. A voiceless scream sounded in her throat, darkness overtaking her.

Then she was running ...

7

As Delaney pulled a slice of bread from the toaster and slathered on a pat of butter, she cast a surreptitious glance at Corbin who was at the table eating a bowl of cereal. Remnants of her dream the night before swirled around her, making her feel a sense of embarrassment. *Geez.* The dream had felt so real, like they'd actually kissed. She shook her head, willing herself to get a grip. It was only a dream, after all.

A guy had brought over Corbin's luggage. Freshly showered, he wore a faded pair of jeans and snug black t-shirt that stretched over his wide shoulders, revealing the outline of his very defined pecs. Just as she'd suspected, he was a casual-clothes guy. His messy hair was still damp, and there was a faint sleep line along the edge of his right eye. She bit back a smile. He was darn cute and so very masculine at the same time. His presence filled her entire condo, making her keenly aware of him every second.

What she should've been thinking about, however, was her show tonight. She had to be at the top of her game. But that was hard, considering she'd hardly gotten any sleep. Aside from the stupid dream, every time she heard a noise, it sent terror racing over her. Several times last night, she'd been tempted to go into Corbin's room and sleep on a pallet, just so she wouldn't have to be alone. The only thing that kept her from doing it was pride. She didn't want him to think she was throwing herself at him. It was embarrassing enough that he'd caught her checking him out at the party. And he'd certainly not hesitated to call her on it. She didn't want to add fuel to that fire.

She took her plate and sat down at the table across from him. *Act normal*, she commanded herself. *Don't think about how the very sight of this man quickens your blood and starts the butterflies flapping in your stomach.* This was a job for Corbin. Nothing else. She'd do well to remember that.

He pushed aside his empty cereal bowl and leaned back in his seat. "Let's go over the plans for the next few weeks."

She took a bite of toast, collecting her thoughts. "The main thing I have going this month is my album." She told him about having to have the songs written and recorded by the end of the month. Then she rattled off a few other engagements. "Two months from now, I'm going on tour."

He nodded. "Tell me about your ex-husband."

She coughed, causing a crumb to get lodged in her throat. She reached for her glass and took a few gulps. She coughed again more forcefully this time, trying to clear her throat. Finally, she got the crumb to go down. Her cheeks went warm, then scalding hot when she saw the amusement in Corbin's eyes, which were more gold than green today.

"Do I need to give you mouth-to-mouth?"

Her eyes popped. "No, that won't be necessary."

"Too bad," he uttered in an intimate tone that sent tingles circling down her spine. She had to resist the urge to fan her face. *Sheesh.* She was blushing like a school girl. And from the look of his coy smile, he knew the effect he had on her. She sat up straight in her seat, trying to get a handle on herself. How was it that she could perform in front of thousands of people, then fall to pieces because Corbin asked her a simple question? "Why do you want to know about Tuck?"

"The more I know about Tuck and Hugh, the better."

His voice was light, casual. But underneath the façade, she detected a keen interest. Or maybe she was reading too much into things. How much did she want to tell him? She didn't like telling anyone about her relationship with Tuck, but she especially didn't want to tell Corbin. There was an unreadable expression on his rugged features as he waited for her to expound. She shifted in her seat. The best way around this was to stick with the facts. "I met Tuck when I was sixteen years old. I never knew my father. My mother and I lived in a trailer park in Noble, Alabama. Hugh was our landlord." She wasn't about to tell Corbin that her mother and Hugh had a thing ... even though her mother was ten years his senior. If Corbin wanted that bit of sordid information, he'd have to search it out himself. "Tuck and I got married when I was nineteen."

"You were really young," he mused.

"Yes." She could tell he wanted her to say more, but she just sat there.

He rubbed his ear. "Why did you and Tuck get divorced?"

She tensed. "Is this really necessary?" He was her bodyguard, not her psychiatrist.

"I need to get the full picture. Any seemingly insignificant detail might prove useful." His eyes probed hers with such intensity that it burned into her soul, stripping her bare. She knew for sure in that moment that Corbin's interest in her past went beyond a professional level. He was interested in her, the same way she was interested in him. Their strong connection made little sense, but it was there nevertheless.

She ran through the options of things she could disclose. Her stomach churned as she thought about the beatings and how she'd ended up in the hospital, broken and battered. It was humiliating. Certainly not something she wanted to tell Corbin. She realized he was studying her. Then she caught something in his eye. Her hospital stay was public record. She held him with a look. "You already know, don't you?"

He didn't flinch. "Yes."

The hair on the back of her neck rose as she clenched her teeth.

What was this? Some sort of game? Or test? "Then why're you asking me?"

"Because I want to hear it from you." He paused. "I want to understand how someone like you could've ended up with him."

Her back went ramrod straight when she caught the accusation in his tone. The defense she'd spent years building screamed in her mind. *Because I was young ... stupid. Desperate. The only daughter of a mother who was an alcoholic and druggie. I felt trapped and alone, then Tuck stepped into the picture. Ironic that the very person I thought would rescue me ended up being my undoing.*

But she wouldn't tell Corbin any of that. She'd hold the anger close the way she always did, putting on a good face for the world. That was the only hope she had of surviving this. The world knew her as Delaney Mitchell. Delores Millstead died a long time ago. She grunted, giving him a hard look. "To answer your question, I wish I knew why I ended up with Tuck. That's the million-dollar question." She tucked her hair behind her ear, pushing away her plate, no longer hungry.

He assessed her with thoughtful eyes. Finally, he sat back, crossing his arms over his chest. "Nope. I don't buy it."

Her brows scrunched. "What?" The nerve! Corbin didn't even know her. He had no right to judge her.

"You know why you married Tuck. I can see it in your eyes." He leaned forward. "But you won't let anyone in, will you?"

Blood pounded against her temples. How in the heck could he read her so well? She let out a harsh chuckle. "All right wise guy ... let's talk about you. What skeletons do you have in your closet?" She saw it, that slight twitch in his eyes that let her know he was harboring secrets too. Then the mask came down as a smile tugged at his lips. "There's that bite I saw last night at the bar. I knew the fighter was in there."

She couldn't help but laugh. "Yeah, I'll fight, but I don't know how much good it'll do me," she said dryly. She'd fought Tuck for all it was worth ... had thought she was finally out of his grasp ... until Hugh showed up. Now things were infinitely worse than they'd been with Tuck. At least Tuck loved her in his twisted way. Hugh was dispassionate, analytical. He'd gut her like a fish, then toss her aside without a second thought. She'd witnessed firsthand what happened when people tried to go up against Hugh Allen. Those people disappeared, and often, their families did as well. A shiver went down her spine as she hugged her arms.

"You'll need that fight," Corbin continued. "I have a feeling this thing will get ugly before it's over. From what I've learned about Hugh, he's ruthless."

"You have no idea," she muttered. "Hugh has no regard for moral decency. No appreciation for human life." Moisture rose in her eyes as she thought of her mother and how Hugh had destroyed her.

Corbin placed a hand over hers, sending electricity zinging through her. For a split second, all she could think about was his touch, how his skin felt against hers. She felt protected and invigorated at the same time.

"I give you my word that I'll keep you safe."

She nodded, unable to stop a tear from rolling down her cheek. Could Corbin really keep her safe? She could tell from the fierce look in his eyes that he believed he could. But he'd never met Hugh face-to-face. Maybe Hugh would destroy Corbin too. Her heart cried at that. No, she couldn't think this way. Couldn't let fear take hold.

He offered a reassuring smile. "I promise."

The confident timber of his voice resonated in her chest, sending a wave of comfort over her. Maybe he could really help. In that moment, despite everything, she realized she was glad Corbin Spencer was here. She looked at their hands, panic slicing ribbons through her. She couldn't get involved with Corbin, no matter how attracted to him she was. She was about to snatch her hand away, but his phone buzzed. He removed his hand from hers and answered it on the second ring.

No *hello*, simply, "Hey, Sutton." She tensed when a shadow slipped over Corbin's features. "I understand." Corbin glanced at her. "I'll tell her." He ended the call with a heavy sigh.

"Tuck's dead, isn't he?" she managed to squeak.

"Yes."

Tears spilled down her cheeks. The room began to spin as her throat closed. She coughed, trying to get a good breath, but the suffocating panic was too thick to break through.

Corbin rushed to her side. "Are you okay?"

She stumbled to her feet. "He'll come for me." She had to get out of here ... had to do something ... but what?

Corbin put his arms around her. "I'm here."

A sob rose in her throat as she buried her head in his shoulder and wept. Tears for Tuck whom she'd once loved. And tears for herself, for what lay ahead.

CORBIN SCOWLED when he saw the throng of reporters gathered in front of the recording studio, awaiting their arrival. He glanced sideways at Delaney who had her game-face on. Her make-up and hair were as perfect as any Southern Diva he'd ever seen, no trace of tears. He had to hand it to Delaney. She'd allowed herself a good cry on his shoulder, then pulled herself together and announced that she was keeping to her normal schedule. "I have an album to complete," she said, squaring her jaw. "And I refuse to let the Allen brothers take one more thing from me. If Hugh wants a fight, then by golly, a fight is what he'll get."

While Corbin admired Delaney's determination and spunk, he wondered if she should cancel tonight's event with the senator. At the mere mention of the idea, Delaney went on a rampage. The woman was more stubborn than a moose. Corbin would simply have to do the best he could under the circumstances. The party was at six, with Delaney scheduled to perform at seven. Sutton's security guys were going to the Senator's home at 2 p.m. to do a thorough sweep of the area, make sure it was secure before Delaney's arrival.

For the first time since he'd left the SEALs, Corbin wished he had a better relationship with his former comrades in Team 7. Had a one of them been present tonight, Corbin would've felt better. He was tempted to call Cannon to see if he could come. He and Cannon had a decent relationship, but not good enough to call on him last minute. No, he'd have to rely on Sutton's security guys and his own prowess, hoping that would be enough. The good news was that Sutton had outfitted his SUV with an arsenal of firearms. Corbin was well prepared in that aspect.

He pulled the SUV alongside the curb and glanced in the rearview mirror at Anton. "You ready?"

Anton nodded. Technically, his shift ended a couple of hours ago, but when he learned about Tuck's death and how the threat was now elevated, he agreed to accompany Delaney and Corbin to the studio. The plan was for Corbin to escort Delaney in the building while Anton parked the SUV.

Corbin's senses went on full alert as he touched the Glock 19 pistol tucked in his belt over his right hip. He turned to Delaney. "You ready?"

She pushed her purse strap over her shoulder, her jaw tightening. "Yep."

The reporters circled around Corbin as he got out of the SUV and hurried around to get Delaney. He paused before opening her door, his eyes scouring the road and surroundings, looking for any signs of a shooter. From what he could tell, the coast was clear. He put an arm around Delaney as they walked quickly towards the building.

A microphone was shoved in Delaney's face. It was mass confusion, questions pelting them from every direction.

"How do you feel about your ex-husband's death?"

"Do you feel responsible?" This came from a pretty reporter, her demeanor aggressive.

Delaney's face was rigid, her eyes fixed straight ahead.

Corbin wanted to knock the vultures out of the way. Unable to do that, he gave them death glares instead. Not that it did any good.

"Will you still perform tonight at Senator Fleming's birthday party?"

"Will you be attending Tuck's funeral?"

"Is your upcoming tour cancelled?"

Corbin opened the door to the studio and they stepped in, leaving the pack of wolves outside. He felt Delaney's shoulders sag in relief as they walked deeper into the building. Corbin also breathed a sigh of relief. *So far so good.*

Now, if they could just get through tonight, they might be okay.

8

Restless currents of energy buzzed through Delaney as she looked at her reflection in the mirror. Her brown eyes were muddy, filled with fear, her skin pale beneath the makeup. Was Hugh out there in the crowd of people, waiting to exact his twisted form of justice?

She heard a tap at the window. Her heart leapt in her throat as she whirled around, her hand going over her chest. She laughed, feeling a weak relief, when she realized the sound was rain splattering against the glass. She turned again to face the mirror. A guest room in the Senator's home had been converted into a dressing room. She was set to perform in one hour. It was comforting to know that Corbin was right outside the door. He'd asked if she wanted him to come into her dressing room after she got changed into her stage clothes, but she told him she needed a few minutes alone to mentally go over the set. When Corbin was around, it was hard to focus on anything but him. Right now, she needed to focus on the performance.

Today, at the recording studio, she'd felt Corbin's eyes on her as he sat outside the glass booth. Several times, when they made eye contact, he gave her an encouraging nod, which was more comforting than Delaney wanted to admit. She couldn't believe she was forming such a strong connection with someone she hardly knew. Maybe it was time she turned the tables and asked Corbin a few personal questions, see what kind of man he really was. Then again, she didn't trust her own judgement. Tuck had fooled her. Why couldn't Corbin?

A knock sounded once before the door opened. She looked up as her hairstylist Gina rushed in.

"Sorry I'm late," she blustered. "Traffic was a beast." She hurried over to Delaney and air-kissed her cheek before dumping her items on the nearby bed.

Delaney smiled. Gina was always a bundle of nerves. To the point where Milo questioned if Delaney should find someone else. Delaney had no intention of starting over with another stylist. She loved what Gina did with her hair, how she could make it look glamorous without weighing it down with an excessive amount of hairspray. And, besides, Gina's nervous demeanor helped distract Delaney from her own anxiety.

Tonight, Gina's round face was beet red, her hair windblown and damp from the rain. Delaney could tell she'd been rushing to get here.

"Is it raining hard outside?"

"Yes, it's horrible." She wrinkled her nose. "And I forgot my umbrella." She waved a hand. "Oh, well. C'est la vie." Her hand went to her hip as she jutted her thumb at the closed door. "Who's the hunk outside?"

Gina was notorious for switching topics midstream. Delaney sputtered out a laugh. "W—what?"

"You know the guy I'm talking about. The one parked outside your door. He's gorgeous. Those intense eyes, perfect body." She clucked her tongue, her eyes dancing wickedly. "Is he real?"

A giggle bubbled in Delaney's throat. She was glad she wasn't the only one so taken with Corbin. "He's my new bodyguard."

"Well, he's got my vote," Gina said, then trilled her tongue. "I wouldn't mind having someone like him guarding me." She frowned.

"If I didn't have fourteen rowdy kids, a husband, two dogs, and a fish, that is."

Delaney laughed. Gina was happily married to a great guy with three boys, but she often joked that it felt more like fourteen.

"Okay, enough about Captain America. We need to make this quick."

Now that she thought about it, Corbin did kind of look like Captain America, maybe with a little rebel mixed in—Captain America meets Iron Man. Yes, definitely Iron Man with Corbin's messy hair and keen wit.

"You doing okay?"

"Yes, why?" Delaney asked reflexively, then saw the look of compassion in Gina's eyes.

"I heard about your ex. I'm sorry, I know it can't be easy."

The familiar tension settled like a rock in Delaney's stomach. "No, it's not," she said, clenching her hands. Gina didn't know the half of it. No one did, except for Milo, Sutton Smith, and Corbin.

"If you need someone to talk to, I'm here."

"Thanks."

Gina turned to the bed, opened the latch on the metallic blue suitcase and lifted the lid. She pulled out a flat iron and blow dryer, along with a dozen or more hair products, which she placed on the table beside Delaney. She took a quick assessment of Delaney's red blouse. Rhinestones dotted the top section. The bottom edge was cut at an angle, swooping down in a triangle on Delaney's right side, long fringe hanging over her jeans. The final touch was the red leather cowboy boots.

Gina pursed her lips. "I think we should do your hair down tonight, but big with loose curls." She glanced at the rhinestone earrings on the table. "We'll need to push the sides of your hair back to showcase those babies."

"Sounds good to me." Delaney spotted a narrow, silver package wrapped in a matching bow. About two feet long, it was beside Gina's purse. "What's that?"

Gina slapped her forehead. "I'm glad you said something. I'm such a twit. A delivery man handed it to me right as I got here. It's for you." She handed Delaney the box.

Delaney took it, trying to decide if she should open it or call Corbin to check it out.

Gina gave her a funny look. "Are you okay? You look a little pale."

She forced a smile. "Yeah, it's just been rough ... with Tuck's death."

"I know. I was surprised you didn't cancel tonight."

"Believe me. I thought about it, but this is such a great opportunity. I couldn't afford to pass it up."

Gina nodded in understanding. "That's the nature of this business, honey. You've gotta pay those dues before you can take a breather."

"Yep," Delaney mumbled, her focus on the package. A sense of foreboding trickled over Delaney as she looked at it. She was about to say that she needed to get Corbin when Gina reached for it.

"Look at you ... all shy about a secret admirer." She rumbled out a deviant chuckle. "I'll open it. It's probably the closest I'll ever come to a secret admirer. Also, we're running out of time. I'll need at least thirty minutes to do your hair justice."

Delaney held her breath as Gina untied the bow. She lifted the lid, smiling. "It's a rose," she announced. Then her expression grew perplexed. "A black rose." Her features tightened, her lips going down in a frown. "There's a note, with red splotches on the edges."

Red splotches of blood. Somehow Delaney managed to speak. "What does it say?"

Gina's voice trembled. "Blood always remembers."

AT THE SOUND of Delaney's shrill cry, Corbin sprang from his seat and ran full speed into the room. His hand went to his Glock as he scoured the room. "What's wrong?"

Terror ringed Delaney's eyes as she pointed to the box on the bed.

The hairstylist was standing beside Delaney shaking her head back and forth. She also looked petrified.

Corbin's pulse raced as he peered into the box. A single black rose.

The stylist pointed to the square of white paper on the bed. Corbin only had to glance to discern the blood splatters. He read the note, then looked at Delaney.

"Where did this come from?" He'd done a sweep of the dressing room before Delaney entered.

"Someone gave it to Gina on her way into the mansion."

"A delivery man," Gina added.

"Why didn't you come and get me?" He glared at Delaney, not trying to hide the frustration in his voice.

"I was going to—"

"But I grabbed it and opened it," Gina finished. She spread her hands. "I had no idea what was inside. I assumed it was from a secret admirer." Her voice dribbled off to silence.

The thought of what could've happened rolled over Corbin like a semi-truck. "This could've been a bomb!" He raked a hand through his hair, exhaling loudly. He'd been sitting outside the door, assuming everything was fine. Then the stylist waltzed in with a package. He looked at the middle-aged, heavy-set woman with the ruddy complexion. She seemed harmless enough, but one could never be sure.

Delaney's face drained as she bit down on her lower lip. "I'm sorry. Everything happened so fast."

"Who was the delivery man?" Corbin demanded.

Gina drew back. "I—I don't know."

"What did he look like?"

"Muscular ... young ... closely-cropped, brown hair."

"What was he wearing?"

"Gray delivery clothes."

"Anything else you can tell me?"

Gina looked at the door like she wanted to dart out of it. "Um, he had a tattoo on his wrist."

"What kind?"

"Some type of line." She hugged her arms, looking at Delaney as an explanation gushed out. "I was in a hurry and didn't pay much attention."

He glared at the woman. Her lower lip trembled like she might break into tears, but he wasn't about to cut her any slack. Not if it meant putting Delaney at risk. He surveyed Delaney. "How well do you know her?"

Delaney's eyes bugged. "Gina?"

"Yes."

"Very well." Delaney flashed Gina an apologetic look as she touched the woman's arm. "She didn't have anything to do with this, Corbin."

"You're darn tootin' I didn't," Gina retorted, her face going red. She rolled her eyes. "I appreciate him wanting to keep you safe, but Captain America needs to take it down a notch."

Corbin made a face. "What?" When Delaney's cheeks turned pink, he realized they'd been discussing him. He didn't know if he should be flattered or insulted. At any rate, they had more pressing matters to deal with right now.

Delaney started trembling, tears pooling in her eyes. "He's coming for me."

A wild look came into Gina's eyes. "Who?"

"Tuck's brother Hugh. He said if Tuck died," her voice choked, "he'd kill me." Hysteria coated Delaney's voice, and Corbin could tell she was on the verge of losing it.

Gina's jaw dropped, fear creeping into her eyes. "What's going on here?"

Corbin wasn't about to explain himself to this woman. "Could you please step outside? I need to talk to Delaney alone."

Gina turned to Delaney. "Really? He's ordering me out? I don't want to leave you alone with him." She glared at Corbin.

"It's okay." Delaney flashed a wan smile. "Really."

Gina straightened her shoulders, giving Corbin a look that said,

Go jump in a lake. "I'll be right outside," she clipped as she marched out, closing the door behind her.

"Are you all right?" Corbin asked, going to Delaney's side.

Tears rolled down her cheeks. A self-deprecating laugh crackled through her throat as she swiped her tears with her palms. "I don't know." The haunted look in her eyes cut Corbin to the quick. "Do you think Hugh's here?" she asked hoarsely.

He let out a breath. "It's a possibility." He sat down on the edge of the bed facing her. He leaned forward so they'd be eye-to-eye. "We knew this could happen, which is why we requested extra security."

She nodded, biting down on her lower lip. "You're right," she finally said. "I knew this was coming." Her voice caught. "But the rose ... and the note ... it makes it a thousand times worse." She clenched her hands, her lips vanishing into a tight line.

Corbin wanted to gather Delaney in his arms and whisk her away from the danger. "You don't have to go through with the concert tonight." He saw her hesitation, could tell she wanted to flee. But then she tightened her jaw. "No, I'm done running. Cancelling this show wouldn't bode well for my reputation." Her voice gathered confidence as she continued. "I'm doing the show."

"You sure?" While he applauded her courage, he didn't want anything bad to happen to her. Protecting her while she was on stage in front of hundreds of people wouldn't be easy. His mind ran through the protocols which were in place. Senator Fleming had his own security team, and they were supposedly checking the credentials of every guest prior to entry. Also, Sutton's guys were here, along with Anton. Still, there was a large margin for error. There would be no way to guarantee Delaney's safety. She seemed to be reading his thoughts.

"It's okay. I know the risks."

He searched her face. "You sure?"

She lifted her chin. "Yes."

He touched her arm. "I promise, I'll be by your side the whole time."

A strained smile stretched over her lips. "For better or worse, huh?"

"For better or worse," he repeated.

9

Corbin positioned himself off to the side of the stage, near the front of the ballroom. It was hard to concentrate on keeping Delaney safe when she was so dang intoxicating—fire and dynamite. Her voice had a rich, full sound with a hint of the huskiness he found so alluring. The lyrics flowed out of her effortlessly as she leaned into the microphone stand to sing. It wasn't just that she had an incredible voice, but also a compelling presence that captured the attention of everyone present. She was gorgeous, her long blonde hair shimmering against the lights. Her outfit accentuated her curves as she swayed to the music. Every time she leaned her head back, he caught a glimpse of her dangling earrings. He let his gaze linger on her shapely legs and fire-engine red, cowboy boots. Finally, he pulled his eyes away from her and back to the crowd. No wonder Delaney was on the cusp of stardom. No one could resist her.

His eyes moved over the guests, mostly high-class, smooth-talking politician types with beautiful women adorning their arms like trophies. Senator Fleming and his wife were seated in the center of the front row. Corbin recognized at least two security personnel sitting nearby, dressed in tuxedos to blend in with the guests.

At least, most everyone was seated. It made it easier to keep track of people. A wait staff dressed in black and white uniforms threaded through the rows, serving drinks and appetizers. Delaney would perform for thirty minutes, then end with *Happy Birthday*, at which time an enormous cake lit with sparklers would be wheeled out.

Corbin spotted Milo, Delaney's manager, three rows back. Milo caught his gaze and offered a slight nod. The man was understandably tense. They'd spoken earlier outside Delaney's door. Milo expressed his appreciation and relief that Sutton had agreed to represent Delaney. Then he questioned if Corbin could really keep Delaney safe here tonight. Corbin had answered honestly that he'd do his best, but couldn't guarantee anything. There were too many aspects beyond his control. Then again, no matter how thoroughly you planned for a situation or how skilled you were, things could always go wrong. He knew that better than anyone.

No group was more prepared than SEAL Team 7 to go into that Filipino village to rescue the diplomat and his family. And yet, they didn't count on one of their informants betraying them. By the time they realized it was an ambush, it was too late. And Doug was killed.

Goosebumps prickled over Corbin's skin. Would that happen here? Would Hugh Allen get to Delaney? He squared his jaw, pushing aside the fears, knowing they weren't helping. The only way he could keep Delaney safe was to remain vigilant. He scoped the crowd with a practiced eye, glancing across the room at Anton, who was doing the same. Corbin picked out the security team, sitting in strategic locations around the room. Security had checked the I.D.s of every guest in attendance. Everything should be fine.

And yet, it didn't feel fine. The air reeked of impending doom. Something was about to happen. Corbin could feel it.

FUNNY that with all these people here Delaney would be so tuned in to Corbin. His jaw was stone, his eyes perpetually scanning the crowd. He exuded such a magnetic energy that she was surprised all eyes in the room weren't drawn to him instead of her. No wonder she'd noticed him last night at the party. He was a walking poster in jeans, a white-collar shirt, and dark gray sports coat. Corbin Spencer was the kind of guy who could step on heads and make things happen. She could tell he took his job seriously and felt safer with him here. She jerked when she fumbled slightly over the last few lines of her song. Time to shift her focus from Corbin to the performance.

She flashed a bright smile taking hold of the microphone. "How y'all doing tonight, folks?" she boomed.

The crowd roared in response. Normally, she felt invigorated when she was performing, plugged into the energy of the crowd. But tonight, she was too tense to completely lose herself.

Keep the energy going, Delaney. "This next one's a favorite. It's called *Blue Skies and Rolling Hills,* written about my home state Alabama, the beautiful." Applause sounded throughout the room. She reached for her guitar leaning close by, then placed the strap over her shoulder. She'd done a few fast songs. This was slower, allowing her a chance to catch her breath. After this, she'd do one more fast song, then sing *Happy Birthday.* It was almost over. She just had to soldier on to the finish line.

THE SONG about Alabama evoked a twinge of nostalgia, reminding Corbin of the fondness he felt for Colorado. Especially Birchwood Springs where he'd grown up. He thought of his grandfather Wallace, the most stubborn man on the planet. His heart clutched as he thought of his beloved grandmother Lou Ella who was in a care center being treated for Alzheimer's. She'd been more of a mother than grandmother to Corbin, and it tore him up inside that she didn't recognize anyone, didn't even know her own identity. She was a prisoner inside her own mind.

His thoughts went to his sister Adelaide, or Addie. Two years younger, Addie was feisty, outspoken and mad as a trapped wasp that he'd left Birchwood Springs. Addie somewhat forgave him for joining the Navy. But when he left again, only a few weeks after retiring from the SEALs, Addie went on a rampage, accusing him of deserting the family and leaving her holding the bag to look after their grandparents. Addie was right. He should've stayed, but he couldn't stand being back there—not with Gram in a care center and his conscience railing about all the things he should've done differently. He had to get away, lose himself in the commotion of a bigger city. Unfortunately, there was no place far enough or big enough to escape from himself.

Working for Sutton gave him a new lease on life. And the fact that he was intensely attracted to Delaney added another layer. Whether that layer was good or bad he didn't know. At any rate, Corbin had a second chance to prove he wasn't a total screw-up, and he was going to do his best to step up to the task.

He looked at Anton whose eyes were fixed on a female server a few rows back. Something about the woman was off. What was it? He took an assessment. She seemed tense like she was about to spring into action. An older man waved to get the server's attention, but she ignored him, keeping her gaze trained on Delaney. Anton must've noticed it too, which is why he was watching her so intently

Alarm bells trilled through Corbin. He turned his head and spoke into the tiny microphone on his coat collar, which patched him into the network of security guards. "Female server in the center, three rows back," was all he had time to say before the woman tossed aside the tray to reveal a gun.

Corbin acted reflexively, drawing his pistol and firing. Before joining the SEALs, Corbin had been a good marksman, but with the added training, he rarely missed. The bullet hit the woman square in the chest. The force jerked her back as she let out a strangled cry, her hand going to her chest, a circle of blood spilling out from the wound. It raced through Corbin's mind that the woman had gotten off a shot before she went down. He looked at the stage, relieved to see that Delaney was okay. Murmurs rustled through the group as people scattered like frightened sheep. The senator's security detail surrounded him and his wife, huddling them out of the room.

Corbin heard another shot. Delaney went to the floor. His heart dropped. Had she been shot or was she taking cover? This shot was fired from a male server in the back. Before the man could shoot again, Anton fired, but missed. Another security guard shot, dropping the man to his knees. Amidst the chaos of the frantic guests, several members of Sutton's security team moved in to apprehend the shooters. Corbin pushed his way to the stage, his only thought to get to Delaney.

It took him less than a minute to reach her, but it felt like an eternity. He was relieved that she hadn't been hit. He helped her up, and pushed her behind him, using his body as a shield. "We'll exit through the back," he said gruffly. "Stay back," he ordered the band members. They looked puzzled that Corbin was treating them with suspicion, but nodded, stepping back.

When they got off the stage, he took her hand. "Let's go." They ran for the back exit where the SUV was parked. All the while, Corbin looked around them, ready to fire should anyone attack.

They'd gone through the plan beforehand. In the event of an incident, Corbin would get to Delaney and they would go out through the kitchen while Anton got the SUV. There were a handful of female servers in the kitchen. When they realized Corbin had a gun, they held up their hands and backed away, faces chalky. "Over there," Corbin ordered, using the gun to motion to the corner. These women didn't look threatening, but he couldn't be sure they weren't in collusion with the other servers. "Keep your hands up," he barked.

When they reached the back door, Delaney was about to push it open and run through, but Corbin caught her collar, pulling her back. "Not yet." For all they knew, the shooters could've been a distraction to send them fleeing out the back into an ambush.

"Do you think Hugh's out there?" The naked fear in her deep brown eyes ignited a fury in Corbin that burned acid through his veins. Everything in him wanted to come face-to-face with Hugh Allen so he could pummel the monster, then bury him. He sucked in a breath, trying to control the anger. He didn't want to lose his head and have a repeat of what happened the night Doug was killed. He had to remain cool, alert. He eased open the door and peered out, noting two things simultaneously. The rain had stopped and the SUV was parked just outside.

"Anton, are you there?" He held his breath, waiting for a response, his mind going through alternate options. Senator Fleming and his wife had been taken to his study, at least that had been the plan. If all else failed, he could take Delaney there until more help arrived.

"I'm here," Anton said.

Relief washed over him. They just had to make it to the SUV, a few steps away. "I've got Delaney. Is the coast clear?"

"Yeah, man, from what I can tell."

"Are you sure? You've got to be right about this. Look around the area. Is there anyone out there?"

"I don't see anybody. It's clear."

Corbin wished again for his former SEAL team members. If they assured him the coast was clear, he could bank on it. "Okay." He'd go with Anton's assessment and pray it was correct. He locked gazes with Delaney whose face was rigid. "You all right?"

She nodded, her lips vanishing into a thin line. His heart bled a little when he saw her clenched fists. She was petrified, but she was a fighter.

"The SUV's right outside. Anton's waiting for us. I'll cover you. Just stay next to me. Be careful though. I'm sure the pavement's slick."

They made it only a couple of steps before a bullet whizzed by Corbin's right ear. "Get down," he yelled, pushing Delaney to the ground. The shot had been fired from across the yard. He crouched down beside Delaney, then saw the shooter partially hidden behind a tree. He aimed and fired a single shot. "Gotcha," he muttered as the man went down. He looked around. There were more of them out there. He spotted one at two o'clock. Another at four o'clock. He fired. Shots came from behind them. He glanced back over his shoulder. Sutton's security guards were returning fire. They had to move now while the snipers were distracted. "Let's go!" They sprinted to the SUV. Corbin yanked open the door and pushed Delaney forward, diving in behind her. "Go!" he yelled as Anton stepped on the gas.

The tires squealed, bullets pinging the windows, as they drove off. Corbin had never been so grateful for bullet-proof glass. He made a mental note to thank Sutton for the SUV.

He turned to Delaney. "You okay?"

She nodded, a stricken expression on her face, as she looked down at her wet clothes. He suspected from the glazed look in her eyes and her shaking hands that she was in shock, but thankfully, she hadn't been shot. He leaned forward, his head going between the seats as he glared at Anton. "I thought you said the coast was clear."

Anton shook his head. "Sorry, man. I thought it was. I had no idea those guys were out there."

Corbin clenched his jaw. "The next time you tell me it's clear, you'd better know it." Had Anton not been driving, he would've finished the brawl they started earlier. And this time, there wouldn't be any security detail to stop him from pounding Anton's head. He gave Anton a long, hard look to let the man know he had his number before sitting back down in the seat.

"Where to, Miss Mitchell? Back to your place?" Anton asked, keeping his eyes on Delaney, not daring to look at Corbin.

Delaney turned to Corbin. "Is it safe?" The words came out screechy, tears gathering in her eyes. "I can't believe this is happening," she muttered, shaking her head and wringing her hands.

Corbin touched her ice-cold hands. "It'll be okay. Look at me," he commanded.

She let out a soft whimper.

"Look at me!"

She turned toward him.

"I'll keep you safe. You have my word."

She searched his face, and even in the near darkness, he could tell she was trying to decide if she could trust him. Finally, she nodded, her shoulders relaxing a fraction.

Anton glanced back at them. "Miss Mitchell, I took the liberty of calling my company. They have a team of bodyguards waiting for us at your condo."

"Thank you, Anton," Delaney said, her voice strained.

"I hope that was okay," Anton continued. "I figured it couldn't hurt to be safe."

Corbin's senses jumped to full alert. When had Anton had time to call his company? There had been scarcely enough time for the man to get out of the mansion to the SUV. Corbin's mind raced through the events of the evening. He'd noticed the server because Anton was watching her. He assumed it was because the woman looked suspicious, but what if it was because Anton was waiting for her to act? Anton told him the coast was clear when there were shooters all over the place. The man had to have noticed something. Had Sutton's security team not come through the back and started shooting, Corbin and Delaney would've been goners.

Delaney's stylist had described the delivery man as muscular with a line tattoo on his wrist. Corbin leaned forward, trying to see, but Anton's wrists were facing the steering wheel. He turned to Delaney and whispered. "How far are we from your condo?" She was about to speak when he put a finger to her lips. "Quietly," he hissed.

She looked puzzled. "About five minutes," she said softly.

His eyes locked with hers. "Do you trust me?"

Concern washed over her as she started blinking. "W—Why? What's happening?"

"No time to explain," he muttered. He whipped out his Glock and pointed it at Anton's head. "Pull over."

Anton's eyes bulged. "Are you crazy, man? I'm on your side." He jerked the wheel, causing them to swerve to the right before he regained control of the SUV.

Delaney gasped, looking at Corbin like he'd lost his mind. "What're you doing?"

"I said pull over!" he repeated, his voice cracking like thunder. He rammed the barrel of the pistol into the back of Anton's head. "I won't ask again."

"All right," Anton blustered. "Miss Mitchell, this guy's crazy."

"You'd better have a good explanation for this," Delaney said through narrowed eyes.

"Turn off the engine," Corbin said when the SUV came to a stop. "Now!"

Anton complied.

"Hands off the wheel."

Anton turned to look at Delaney. "Miss Mitchell, this is ludicrous."

"Turn on the overhead light."

"I knew you were crazy at the bar. I should've busted your pretty face when I had the chance." Anton flipped on the light, his eyes narrowing to black slits.

"Now roll up your sleeves and turn your hands over, palms facing up."

Anton barked out an incredulous laugh. "You're losing it, man."

It was at that moment that understanding registered on Delaney's face. She squared her jaw. "Do as he says."

"Not you too. Fine, palms up. Want me to play patty cake next?" Anton sneered.

"The tattoo that Gina saw. On the deliveryman that gave her the rose," Delaney exclaimed at the same time Corbin saw the tattoo, realizing it was an arrow.

Anton reached for his gun, but Corbin was faster. He jammed the pistol into Anton's head. His voice was controlled, deadly. "Slowly, remove the gun from your holster. No sudden moves. I really don't want to have to splatter your brains in front of the lady," he said morosely. "Drop it on the seat," he ordered when Anton held up the gun. He glanced at Delaney. "Get the gun. Do it!" he yelled when she hesitated. She leaned over the seat and grabbed it, then dropped it on the seat beside them like it was a hot coal.

"Now the cell phone." He grabbed it from Anton's hand and placed it on the seat beside him. "How much did Hugh pay you to become a traitor?" Corbin asked, disgust churning in his gut. Hugh had been able to get to Delaney's closest point of contact. No one could be trusted.

"A lot more than your lady back there." Anton rumbled out a

laugh, his voice going vicious. "This world ain't a big enough place for you to hide. He'll find you. You too, pretty boy."

Corbin swore when Delaney sucked in a ragged breath. Stress was taking its toll. Her breathing was shallow and labored, and he feared she might start hyperventilating. Time was ticking away. For all they knew Hugh and his goons could be closing in any minute.

He pointed the gun at Anton's head. "Drive us to Sutton's mansion. Any funny movements and you die!"

10

After a decent night's sleep at Sutton's mansion, Delaney was feeling somewhat better about her situation. Granted, she was still freaked out, and if she thought about it too much, her whole body would start to shake. On the upside, it was comforting to have Corbin by her side. Those first few moments when he put the gun to Anton's head, she thought he was nuts. But if he hadn't realized Anton was leading them into a trap, they'd be dead right now.

Delaney had no doubt that the security detail Anton referred to, the ones waiting at her condo, were Hugh and his men. A shiver ran down her spine. How long could they keep evading Hugh? Were they just postponing the inevitable? And now, it was not only her life at risk but also Corbin's. She hugged her arms, shaking off the fears. Better to try and focus on the positive.

They were in Corbin's SUV, headed to a shop to pick her out a wig. Corbin glanced sideways at her. "You okay?"

An automatic smile plastered over her face—the one she used on stage to suppress the jitters. "Yeah."

"You're a terrible liar."

She turned in surprise. "What?"

He glanced at her hands. "You keep digging those fingernails into your palms and we're gonna have to get a set of pliers to pull them out."

She looked down, realizing she was clenching her hands. "Oh." She opened her hands, which felt stiff from the tension.

"You know, you'd be a whole lot prettier if you'd smile once in a while."

Her eyes widened, then she laughed, recognizing the lyrics of a popular song. "'Lullaby' by Shawn Mullins."

"Yep." A smile slid over his lips giving him a boyish, mischievous appearance that was even harder to resist than his usual tough-guy expression. She allowed herself a moment to check him out. Her eyes slid over his rugged profile, the defiant set of his chin, his defined biceps, even more pronounced with him holding the steering wheel, his chiseled abs. She noted how the t-shirt and jeans seemed to be an extension of him.

A dart of warmth shot through Delaney with enough force to heat the whole West Coast. *Sheesh.* Crazy that she'd be thinking about how good-looking Corbin was in the middle of a crisis. She angled toward him, curious to know more about the man who was throwing her for a loop and making her rethink her stance on steering clear of a relationship. "Are you a fan of folk rock?"

"I like all types of music. Rock, jazz, country."

She pursed her lips. "Hmm ... a man with eclectic tastes. Impressive."

A hint of a smile pulled at his lips. "I'm glad you find something about me impressive. I was starting to wonder."

The comment broadsided her, rendering her speechless. There were many things she found impressive about Corbin Spencer, hence the problem. She could tell from his sly expression that he was teasing her, which helped relax her a little.

He glanced at her. "You were amazing last night, by the way."

The compliment settled into her chest like a warm ray of sunshine. "Thanks." Of all the people in the audience, she'd been most aware of him. It was gratifying to know that he'd paid attention to her performance.

"You have such a unique voice. Where did you learn to sing like that?"

"My mother loved to sing. From the time I was a kid, she was always strumming on her guitar and singing ... mostly Top 50 Billboard hits. She taught me to play the guitar and would get me to harmonize with her." Those were some of the few happy memories Delaney had of her mother—before she became so addicted to drugs that she couldn't function. One of the darkest days of Delaney's life was the day her mother sold her guitar to buy drugs. But she wasn't going to tell Corbin that.

"What was your mother's name?"

"Angie."

"Tell me about her." Corbin's voice was gentle, patient. Still, it touched a nerve.

Her jaw tightened as she balled her fists again. "What do you already know about her?"

"Facts, mostly that Sutton gave me."

She remained silent, waiting for him to expound. Why was she still so dang sensitive where her mother was concerned? Maybe she should just get it out in the open so it wouldn't be hanging between them. She felt like she was on a high dive, trying to decide if she should go into the water gently or just plunge right in. "My mother was an alcoholic and druggie," she blurted. "She never could hold down a steady job, so we lived off food stamps and what little we could scrape together. Sometimes, when we got desperate, she'd sing at a local bar for a few extra bucks. Unfortunately, she drank up the profits before it did us much good." Resentment sat like lead on her chest as she stared unseeingly at the road in front of them.

"I'm sorry."

She nodded. "Thanks." How many times had she heard those two empty words from well-wishers?

"Tell me about your mother's relationship with Hugh."

A surprised laugh gurgled in her throat. "You don't pull any punches, do you?"

He shrugged. "I don't have time to pull it out of you diplomatically. I need to know what type of person we're dealing with."

The words tumbled out like bricks against a cement floor. "A manipulator, a devil with a black heart. The meanest man I've ever laid eyes on."

"So your mother and Hugh were romantically involved?"

Her hand went to her throat. "There was nothing romantic about it. But yes, they were involved." She spat out the words like they were poison. "Even though my mother was ten years older than Hugh, she was beautiful ... looked about the same age as him. Hugh was our landlord. We never had money to pay the rent. I'll let you figure out the rest." The beginning of a headache formed across the bridge of her nose. "How much farther to the wig store?" She was ready to be out of the SUV to give her space from Corbin and his probing questions.

"About ten more minutes."

Delaney turned away from Corbin and looked out the window, letting her mind get lost in the passing buildings. The plan was for them to get Delaney a wig, then drive thirteen hours to Birchwood Springs, Colorado, the small town Corbin was from. Corbin insisted on going there because he was familiar with the terrain and people. Sutton contacted Milo, letting him know that Delaney was being moved to an undisclosed location and would remain there until the situation was resolved. Delaney argued that she had an album to record and couldn't lose any time.

"You can't record anything if you're dead," Corbin had said dryly.

He was right, of course. Although it was chilling to hear it put so bluntly. Then again, Corbin wasn't one to mince words. *Obviously!* "But what about my things?" she'd asked. "Can I at least go back to my condo and get them? I'll need my guitar to compose songs." If she was going to be stuffed away in some remote place, she wanted to at least do that. She could get the songs written, then record them all at once. That way, she wouldn't lose too much time.

Corbin had chuckled in amusement. "Are you listening to your-self? Going back to your condo would be a death sentence. Hugh has guys there waiting for you. Heck, for all we know, he could be camped out there himself."

The thought of Hugh Allen or his men invading her personal space, going through her things, sent a shudder through Delaney. She wished she'd never met the Allens. Wished she could run away from this and never look back. *If only.*

In the end, Sutton had a complete wardrobe of clothes in Delaney's size delivered to the mansion, along with a Gibson guitar. He even had a few items delivered for Corbin. Delaney argued that the nominal fee she was paying wouldn't begin to cover the items, but Sutton dismissed her argument with a wave of his hand, telling her not to worry about it. From what Milo said, Sutton helped his girl-friend Leslie and her son, not asking a thing from them. It was obvious that Sutton Smith was not in the security business for money. Whatever his motivations, she was grateful he'd taken her on as a client.

"How did you become a country music star?"

The question jarred Delaney back to the present.

"After Tuck and I got divorced, I took a job at the Bluebird Café as a waitress. My co-workers knew how much I loved to sing. They were always joking that I sounded better than most of the people who took the stage. One evening, a performer had an emergency. I stepped in at the last minute, and a well-known agent Max Gillespie happened to be in the audience and wanted to represent me. Things took off quickly from there. The next thing I knew, I was signing with Montana Crew's record label."

"A rags-to-riches story," he mused. "Do you know what the odds are that you would even get a job at the Bluebird, much less perform there? And then get picked up by an agent? Just like that? Wow. Incredible."

She tucked a strand of hair behind her ear. "I was lucky, I suppose."

"No, you're good. Dang good."

"Thanks." It was surprising how much his approval meant to her. She was just about to launch into a series of questions about his past when he turned into the parking lot of the wig shop.

"We're here." He turned off the engine, a crooked smile tugging at his lips. "Let's see what we can find for you to wear, Delores."

She winced. "Dee," she corrected. She was going to Birchwood Springs under the guise of Corbin's girlfriend. She couldn't use her stage name, so Sutton suggested she go by her real name Delores to keep things simple. She'd thought she'd buried Delores Millstead and didn't relish the idea of digging her up again. But whatever, it was only temporarily. At any rate, she preferred the shortened version of her name.

He grinned. "All right, Dee."

"What?" The intensity of his gaze burned through her. *Sheesh*. It was hard being in such a tight, enclosed space with Corbin Spencer. When he looked at her like that, she could hardly form a clear thought.

"Delaney fits you better."

"Thanks. I agree."

"But I suppose Dee will do, for now."

She reached for her door.

He touched her arm, sending a buzz of awareness through her.

"What?"

"Let me get out first and come around to get you. Just to make sure."

She glanced around, shaking off a shiver. It was only six a.m. They'd passed very few cars on their way over, and there was only one other car in the parking lot, which presumably belonged to the person who ran the shop. "You don't think anyone followed us, do you?" Her voice dribbled off, unease trickling down her spine. Sutton had leaked information to make Hugh believe she was being taken to a safe house in Northern Cal. The hope was that by the time Hugh realized he'd been led on a wild goose chase, she and Corbin would be long gone. She'd even turned her phone over to Sutton for safe keeping, just to make sure Hugh couldn't somehow track her on it.

"No, I don't think we were followed. I watched as we drove and didn't see anyone. But it doesn't hurt to be cautious."

She nodded, biting down on her lower lip.

Corbin came around and opened her door, keeping one hand close to his gun. Her skin crawled as she stepped out of the SUV. The empty air around them felt menacing, like someone could attack any second. She hated this! Feeling so vulnerable. She hated living in constant fear of what Hugh might do! Right after she was released from the hospital, after Tuck's merciless beating that nearly took her life, she promised herself that she'd never cower to Tuck or his brother again. And here she was, running scared.

It wasn't until they stepped through the doors of the shop that Delaney realized she'd been holding her breath. She sucked in air, feeling a little dizzy. Her heart rate spiked when she realized Corbin still had an arm around her. She could feel his fingertips through the thin fabric of her blouse, loved the hardness of his muscular torso against her. Heat rushed to her cheeks as she looked up at him. She cleared her throat. "I'm okay now. You can let go."

Amusement lit his eyes as he grinned. "Pity," he murmured, removing his arm. "I thought we fit together quite nicely."

She wished he'd stop with the innuendos. It was hard enough to remain unaffected by him as it was. But to know that he also liked her ... well, that took the attraction to a whole new level. She traced the outline of his lips, the firm shape of his jaw. Her eyes went to his neck, his prominent Adam's apple so distinctly masculine. Recollections from her dream flooded her. She'd buried her fingers in his spiky hair, felt the delicious sensation of his lips against hers. The kiss had ignited a spark in her powerful enough to start an inferno. But with the all-consuming attraction came something unexpected—the feeling of belonging, of coming to the end of a long journey ... finding the thing she'd searched for her entire life.

Corbin cleared his throat. She jumped slightly, embarrassment cloaking her like a stifling blanket. She'd been standing there, gaping at him. Meanwhile, Corbin and the store clerk were watching her.

She stepped back, putting as much space as possible between her and Corbin.

The woman extended a hand, a professional smile touching her lips. "Hello, I'm Marissa Harris. Let's see what we can help you find. I understand you want something completely different from your real hair."

"Yes." Delaney wasn't sure how much Marissa knew about her situation, but she wasn't about to divulge additional information.

Marissa motioned to a stool beside a mirror. "Have a seat. I have a few selections to get us started."

Delaney sat down.

"Here, put your hair in this." She handed Delaney a hairnet, then reached for a wig. "Let's try this one first." The good news is that with your dark eyes, the brown hair will look natural on you. She fitted the short cap of hair over Delaney's head and adjusted it. Then she stepped back. "What do you think?"

Delaney's first thought was that her hair hadn't been this short since kindergarten. Her second thought was that she looked like she had an animal skin on her head. A laugh bubbled in her throat as she swallowed to stifle it. She looked so ridiculous! Before she could tell Marissa *no*, Corbin spoke up.

"Absolutely not. My woman would never wear that."

This time, she couldn't stop a chuckle from escaping. "Your woman?" She removed the wig and placed it on the counter. Yes, she was going to Birchwood Springs under the guise of Corbin's girlfriend. The tone in his voice sounded so serious, matter-of-fact, that she could almost believe she really was his girlfriend. *Would that be such a bad thing?* Dang these renegade thoughts. *Yes, it would be a bad thing*, she answered, squelching any further thoughts on the subject.

His eyes locked with hers. "Yes, you are my woman."

The certainty in his voice struck a chord inside her. *His woman.* She liked the sound of that. Blood pumped faster through her veins, making a swooshing sound against her temples. She looked at his lips, wondered if they'd feel and taste anything like she'd imagined in her dream. Her voice went higher as she laughed to relieve the tension, her words gushing out. "You sound like the Russian in *Man From U.N.C.L.E.*, where the girl's trying on clothes to pose as his fiancée, and he keeps telling her that his woman wouldn't wear that."

Corbin shrugged. "I assumed girlfriend would do the trick, but I guess we could elevate our situation. Boost you up to fiancée level."

"Girlfriend is good," she said quickly, her cheeks scorching like a sunburn. She swallowed hard, so glad he couldn't read her thoughts. Relieved he didn't know what she'd dreamt about him. Then she caught the mischievous glint in his eyes and realized he was teasing her again, enjoying watching her squirm. And she was rising to the bait. She scooted back in her seat, her chin lifting. *All right, buddy. You wanna play games? Fine. I'll play.* "What would your woman wear?" she asked snippily.

He made a face, his eyes going to the wigs lined up on the counter. "Certainly not those." He looked at Marissa. "No offense."

She waved a hand. "None taken."

Corbin looked thoughtful, his eyes scoping the options. He strode across the room and lifted a copper-brown wig off the mannequin head. "This one."

Delaney wrinkled her nose. "Seriously? You don't think it's too red?"

Marissa tilted her head. "Try it on. It could work. I like the style."

Delaney placed it on her head and pursed her lips, studying her reflection in the mirror. The bangs were wispy, the sides tapering around her face. The length came to her shoulders. Surprisingly, it looked pretty good. She looked like a different woman, yet still attractive. This was good. No one would recognize her with this on.

Marissa stepped up behind her and began fluffing the top. "You can add as much volume as you wish."

"You like it." Corbin quirked a satisfied grin. "I can see it on your face. Admit it."

"You don't know what I'm thinking," she shot back, but couldn't help but smile. "Okay, I do like it." She rolled her eyes. "Who would've guessed ... Captain America's a fashion guru at heart." It was cute how color seeped into his face.

"Is this one a *go*?" Marissa asked.

Delaney looked at Corbin, a thrill shot through her. She liked this energy between them. She'd never been as aware of a man before. "Would your woman wear this?"

His eyes caressed hers. "You're wearing it, aren't you?"

Her breath caught and all she could think about was that his eyes looked more gold than green today. She looked at Marissa who smiled as if to say, *The two of you are great together.*

"Of course, nothing looks as good as the blonde," Corbin continued in a low, throaty tone, "but this will do for now."

Another inference to her being his woman. And he liked her blonde hair. A swarm of butterflies took flight in Delaney's stomach. She looked down to break the connection. *Sheesh.* She was trying to remain aloof around him, dodge the landmines, but she kept tromping right on top of them. These landmines wouldn't destroy her limbs but her heart instead.

"I'll get the care instructions and a special comb," Marissa said, walking into the back.

The attraction was strong even with Marissa in the room. Now that she'd left, it was nearly unbearable. Her fingers itched to pull Corbin close, press her lips to his. She rubbed her hands on her jeans, fighting the temptation.

Corbin leaned back against the counter and folded his arms over his chest. "I guess my fashion sense comes from having a sister."

How was it possible for a guy to look so good in a t-shirt and jeans? She could see the outline of his sculpted abs underneath his shirt. *Focus on what he's saying*, she commanded herself. She fumbled to think of a sensible question. "What's her name?"

"Addie."

"Is she younger or older?" Delaney had always wished for a sister.

"Younger, by two years."

"Do you have any other siblings?"

"Nope, just Addie." He chuckled. "But trust me, she's enough. A fireball. You'll see when you meet her."

She could hear the affection in his voice. It made her a little jealous that she had no one. Then she felt guilty. It wasn't Corbin's fault that her mother had died. Heck, even when her mother was alive, Delaney had been alone. At least now her mother wasn't suffering, and she was free from Hugh's clutches. "Tell me about the rest of your family."

She touched the hair of the wig, fluffing it a little on top. It felt stuffy and constricting on her head, making her skin itch. She wondered if she'd ever get used to it.

"I was raised by my grandparents, Wallace and Lou Ella."

She turned her full attention to him. "What happened to your parents?" A shadow crossed his features, his jaw tightening. She eyed him, waiting for a response. Normally, she didn't make a habit of pushing her way into people's personal space, but Corbin had asked her plenty of uncomfortable questions. *Turnabout is fair play.* Also, she was curious to know more about him.

"My parents died."

"I'm sorry," she said automatically. Then it occurred to her that she was using those same trite words she hated people saying to her. "How?"

His lips drew into a tight line, and she could feel him withdrawing. The two of them really weren't that different. Corbin held his cards close too. She looked him in the eye, a tiny smile curving her lips. "You know about the skeletons in my closet. It should go both ways, right?"

Something shifted in his eyes, and she saw the hint of a smile. "Right." His shoulders relaxed in acceptance. "My parents were on vacation in Mexico and were mugged outside their hotel. Shot and left in the street over a few measly dollars." His eyes went hard, and she saw reflected in them the same sadness that plagued her.

She touched his arm. "I know it sounds hollow, but I really am sorry."

He nodded. "Addie and I were raised by our grandparents."

"I'm excited to meet them." Something flashed in his eyes, giving her the impression she'd said something wrong. "What?"

He rubbed his neck. "My grandmother has Alzheimer's. It's bad. She no longer recognizes anyone."

She caught the slight hitch in his voice. Saw a glimpse of Corbin she'd not seen before—the damaged part of him that spoke to her heart. No wonder she was so drawn to him. He looked at her, an understanding that defied words flowing between them. Like her, he knew what it was like to have his world turned upside down from violence—losing his parents the way he had. And now, he was losing his grandmother too. Her eyes misted as the words rushed out. "No matter how much it hurts, you'll get through it. Just keep moving forward. That's what she'd want you to do."

Tears formed in Corbin's eyes as he nodded and looked away.

"Okay, here we are," Marissa said cheerily, then halted in her tracks, looking back and forth between them. "Oops, am I interrupting something?"

"No," Corbin said, clearing his throat.

Marissa held out a bag. "You're all set. I gave you some special shampoo and an instruction sheet. But let me go over the process with you as well. Make sure you don't have any questions."

Delaney nodded, her mind still on Corbin. Suddenly it hit her that despite the circumstance, she was looking forward to going to Birchwood Springs and getting to know Corbin's grandfather and sister. The more time she spent around Corbin the more intrigued with him she became. Yeah, it wasn't smart to fall for her bodyguard —to fall for anyone, especially with Hugh on her heels. Aside from the danger, her judgement was skewed when it came to men. She didn't want to open herself up to get hurt again. The sensible thing to do would be to forget Corbin and focus on her career. That was her only sure path to safety. But yet, she couldn't seem to help herself. She was so drawn to this man ... had been from the moment she laid eyes on him.

"You ready?" Corbin asked when Marissa finished her spiel.

"Yep."

He motioned with his head. "Let's get on the road."

She sighed. Thirteen hours alone with Corbin Spencer. How in the heck was she supposed to keep her head straight? When they got to the door, he put an arm around her, gathering her into the protection of his muscular body. At his touch, her cells swirled into action, sending heat racing up her neck.

When they stepped outside, an instant change came over him. His jaw went rock hard, his eyes intense as he scoped the area surrounding them. Thrilling didn't even begin to describe this man. He was the type people made movies about ... a rebel, maverick, and Captain America all rolled into one.

His eyes caught hers for one brief moment and he gave her a reassuring smile. Her heart melted as she smiled back. No amount of self-talk would be enough to protect her from Corbin. She was a lost cause for sure.

11

L ittle by little, Delaney was warming up to him. Corbin prided himself on reading people, paid close attention to those little nuances that gave more information than verbal language ever could. Delaney was attracted to him, just as he was to her. But she was fighting against it hard. Corbin couldn't blame her. He'd be paranoid too if he'd been through what she had. Maybe after more time, Delaney would relax around him, realize that he was nothing like Tuck Allen. He tightened his jaw. It rankled his gut to think of Tuck abusing Delaney. And then there was Hugh, the cutthroat killer out for revenge. Corbin would do everything in his power to keep Delaney safe, even if it meant he had to die trying. He couldn't explain it, but Delaney was his responsibility. And now that he'd met her, he'd never be able to let her go. He laughed inwardly realizing how ridiculous that sounded. His grandfather, Wallace, swore that the first time he laid eyes on Lou Ella, he knew they'd be together. Corbin always thought that was wishful thinking, Pops rewriting history to fit with the present. But now, he was starting to wonder if there was something to the story.

Corbin glanced sideways at Delaney. Even with the wig, she was stunning. He was glad they had so much road time so he could get to know her better. And the best part, she couldn't retreat. "So," he began, "if the two of us have any hope of pulling off this boyfriend/girlfriend charade, we need to know details about each other."

The color seeping into her cheeks indicated how uncomfortable she felt about the situation. "What do you want to know?"

"Favorite food."

"Sausage gravy and biscuits," she said without hesitation.

He laughed. "Really? I've never been that crazy about biscuits. They're kind of dry and hard."

She grunted. "That's probably because you've never had a good biscuit. Where did you eat the biscuit that was dry?"

"I dunno, a restaurant."

"Out West?"

"Well, yeah."

"That's the problem. You've never had a Southern biscuit. They're light and flaky, melt in your mouth. I guarantee you that if you have a biscuit made by someone who knows what they're doing, you'll change your mind."

It was fun to see this side of Delaney. Sassy and more carefree. "Do you know how to make biscuits?"

"Of course. I'm Southern, aren't I?"

He chuckled. "Yes, you are." He kept his voice casual, non-threatening. "Maybe you could make me some when we're at the cabin ... see if you can change my mind."

She hesitated for a moment, long enough for him to fear that she'd refuse. "Okay, you're on."

Another win ... little by little. He'd love to have Delaney cook him a meal. Heck, he'd even volunteer to help. Anything to keep her by his side.

"How about you? What type of food do you like?"

"Pasta."

"That's kind of broad. What type of pasta?"

"All types."

"Red sauce or white?"

"Yes."

She laughed. "Okay. What are your hobbies?"

Hobbies? He hadn't thought about that in a long time, not since way before he became a SEAL. "I like target shooting, camping, hiking, snow skiing."

"An outdoor man. I kind of figured that about you."

He could feel her eyes on him. He glanced at her as they shared a smile.

"I always wanted to learn to snow ski." She chuckled. "But in Alabama, the closest thing you get to snow are a few ice storms."

"We'll have to go while we're in Birchwood Springs. There's a resort right next to my grandfather's cabins. My sister works there."

"Really? We could go? Would it be safe? Considering the circumstance ..." Her voice faded into a thick silence.

Corbin wanted this whole ordeal to be over. It cut to hear the dismay in Delaney's tone, to know how terrified she was. He couldn't help it. He reached over and placed a hand over hers. Electricity spiked through him when their skin connected. She had to have felt it too. Yes, he could tell she did ... he knew from the way she went rigid. He thought Delaney might jerk her hand away and was relieved when she didn't. "I think we can manage a trip to the ski resort."

"I'd like that," she said, giving him a wan smile. Carefully, she removed her hand from his. "Sorry, but considering our situation, I'd like to keep things between us professional."

Disappointment pummeled through him as he nodded, putting his hand back on the steering wheel. *One step forward ... two steps back.* He was getting used to Delaney's routine, but he didn't like it.

"How did we first meet? That's the number one question people will ask."

Her comment helped ease some of the tension as he relaxed in his seat, keeping his eyes on the road. "At a party."

"Okay, sounds good to me. What type of party?"

"A fancy shindig on Coronado Island, hosted by a billionaire philanthropist." He saw the surprise on her face. She'd just now figured out the direction he was taking. "I walked into the mansion wearing my new, shiny white tux and felt this gorgeous babe checking me out."

"I was not checking you out," she blustered.

A smile tugged at his lips. "Yes, you were." He cut his eyes at her to let her know she wasn't getting off the hook. She could sit there all day and pretend there wasn't anything between them, but she couldn't deny that she'd noticed him first. "You know it's true."

She made a face. "Fine. I admit it. I was checking you out," she muttered. "What do you want? A confession in blood?"

"I just wanted to hear you say it out loud."

She shoved his arm with a laugh. "You're such a cocky moron. I can't believe you got me to admit that," she uttered.

He glanced at her, not surprised to see her lips turned down in a petulant frown. She was so darn cute that he wanted to pull the SUV over and kiss her right this minute. He chuckled inwardly. Not a good idea. She'd freak out. Never speak to him again. "And then when I went over to talk to you at the bar, you sicked Anton on me."

She chuckled nervously. "Yeah, not one of my finer moments. But you certainly had no trouble holding your own."

The admiration in her voice caused him to lose his train of thought. He fumbled to come up with a response. Did he say *thanks*? Was she complimenting him? Or just stating the facts? Thankfully, she spoke first.

"I'm sorry about the Anton thing. I had no idea you were working for Sutton. I thought you were hitting on me."

He'd dodged this the night before. Time to own up to what really happened. "I was."

She coughed. "Excuse me?"

"I was hitting on you. I didn't realize you were going to be assigned to me. You caught my attention earlier, and I wanted to meet you." There. He'd said it ... gotten it out in the open.

"A-ha! I knew you were hitting on me." Her voice grew animated like she'd just gotten the correct answer on a game show.

His next statement could either move things forward or put a monkey-wrench in them. But he was tired of tiptoeing around the situation. "One minute you openly checked me out and then you shot me down cold when I tried to approach you. Why?" He knew the reason, of course. She was scared because of what happened with Tuck. Still, he wanted to bring it out in the open ... discuss it, hoping they could move past it.

"Because I don't need a relationship right now, especially not with you."

Talk about a punch in the gut. Wow! "What's so bad about me?"

"Never mind. I shouldn't have said anything." She shook her head, angling away from him.

"No, you started this. I wanna hear it." He clutched the steering wheel, awaiting her answer. No way he was going to let her weasel out of this one. She'd given him a personal insult, one which was totally unfounded.

"It's not you. It's me."

"I don't understand."

"Can we just drop it?"

Her voice had a panicked edge. It made him feel for her—how badly she'd been hurt in the past. But he wasn't the bad guy here. All he'd done was try to help her. "No, I don't think we can. I need to know where you're coming from."

She blew out a breath. "Fine. You wanna know why I shot you down?" Her voice went higher. "Well, here it is. I'm attracted to the wrong type of guys."

He tensed. "What makes you so sure I'm the wrong type of guy?"

"Because it's written all over you—your swagger, the intensity you exude like a second set of skin, the rebel." She let out a harsh laugh. "Believe me, I know you, Corbin Spencer. You know how people say they have a knack for finding the most expensive item in the store? Well, that's me when it comes to men. You put ten guys in front of me. Nine of them could be upstanding men and only one the rebel. And I'll pick the menace every time. Guaranteed."

"So, I'm a menace now? Need I remind you that I am one of the good guys?"

"I'm know you're fighting for the right side, and I'm grateful you're in my corner. But tell me, Corbin. Of all the guys Sutton could've picked to protect me, why do you think he picked you to go up against Hugh?"

"Because I'm capable ... have the right set of skills." *Because he wants to give me a second chance to prove I'm not a total screw-up.*

"Because you're as tough and relentless as Hugh. You fight fire with fire, as Sutton said. You put a gun to Anton's head, then asked questions later."

He couldn't argue with that. Doug had told him much the same thing using different words. *"You may be tough,"* he'd said, *"but tough isn't enough. You also have to be tempered."*

From the time he was a kid, Corbin carried around the pain of losing his parents. In his teenage years, that pain turned to a hot anger that fueled him, made him a menace to society ... just as Delaney had accused him of being. Then he met Doug who saw potential in Corbin. Doug made him want to be a better person, set him on the path of becoming more tempered. Corbin thought he was doing better in that regard, right up until the moment Doug was killed and he lost his head. One moment in time, his reckless nature took over. Corbin's actions not only cost him the respect of SEAL Team 7, but also an innocent life. "I'm not a bad person," he muttered, mostly to himself.

"I know."

He jerked slightly, Delaney's comment bringing him back to the conversation at hand.

"I don't mean to accuse you of being a menace. Those are my issues, not yours."

"I know I can be a hothead, but that doesn't make me Tuck. I would never hurt you like he did. And I don't think it's fair that you're trying to hold me responsible for his sins."

"I'm not doing that."

"Okay, then why're you so afraid to admit that there's something between us? I feel it, and I know you do too." He glanced at her. "I can see it in your eyes."

She gulped in a strangled breath. "I beg your pardon," she said stiffly.

"No need to beg," he said pleasantly. "Just answer the question."

She angled toward him. "You get great delight out of pinning me in a corner, don't you?"

He laughed. "I have to admit, pinning you in a corner would have its advantages." He glanced at her, noting how her face had gone cherry red.

"I knew you were trouble from the first minute I saw you," she grumbled, her brows furrowing.

"Seriously? You're talking to the man who saved your life."

"Thank you very much for doing your job," she spat.

"You're welcome." He regretted the words as soon as they left his mouth. A frigid silence settled between them. Delaney was sitting with her arms clamped over her chest, her face rigid.

He sighed. That hadn't gone the way he hoped. He'd known he was probably pushing her too far when he brought up the attraction thing, but he wanted to test the water … break down as many barriers as he could. "I'm sorry. I shouldn't have said that. You don't owe me anything for keeping you safe. Like you said, I was just doing my job." He hated how cold and sterile the words sounded. Yeah, he was working for Sutton, getting paid for the assignment, but this thing with Delaney was personal … more personal than anything had felt in a long time.

"I shouldn't have said that."

It took his brain a second to register that she'd spoken. "Huh?"

"If you'd not realized what Anton was up to, we'd both be dead right now. Thank you. I do owe you my life."

The sincerity in her words caught him off guard. "I'm glad we averted disaster. And that you were safe." He hoped she realized how much he truly meant that.

"About the relationship thing … I can't get involved with anyone right now. Not while this thing with Hugh's hanging over me. Can you understand that?"

He looked sideways, saw the pleading in her eyes, then put his focus back on the road. "Yeah," he finally said. "I understand. But you have to understand that the goal is to make everyone in Birchwood Springs believe you're my girlfriend. So, if I put my arm around you ... hold your hand ... or even kiss you ... you can't freak out." He didn't have to look at her to know she was mortified. She really was fun to tease. Although he was serious. The best way to keep her safe was to make everyone believe they were a couple. Of course, he'd make sure to take every opportunity to kiss her.

"Isn't there some other cover we can come up with? Maybe we're work colleagues?"

"Before I took this job, I was a bouncer at a bar," he said matter-of-factly. "My family knows that's what I was doing. Even if you pretended to be a server at the bar, there's no reason we would travel together, work-wise." He had her and they both knew it.

"Fine," she huffed. "But whatever happens between us will be just for show. You got that?"

"Yep. Loud and clear." He reached for her hand. She snatched it away before he could link his fingers through hers.

"What're you doing?" she demanded.

He grinned. "Practicing."

"Ha! You really are a menace."

He winked. "That's what they tell me."

Her eyes narrowed, but she couldn't stop a smile from spreading over her lips.

That was a good sign. A good sign, indeed. The iceberg was thawing.

It was dark by the time they drove into Birchwood Springs. Corbin looked over at Delaney who was sleeping peacefully, her head resting against the back of the seat. He fought the urge to run his fingers along the curve of her delicate jawline. Interesting that he would feel so attached to Delaney after such a short period of time. There had been a long string of women who'd come and gone in Corbin's life, but no one he was super attached to ... until now. Ironic that the one girl Corbin felt a connection with was determined to keep him at arm's length. He was going to ham up the boyfriend thing for all it was worth and hope that Delaney would come around. She'd already gotten in his head and he had no intention of getting her out. One thing Corbin knew how to do was go after what he wanted, despite all obstacles. There'd be no tapping that brass bell on this one. He was in for the long haul.

Corbin rubbed a hand across his neck and aching shoulders. He was ready to get out and stretch his legs. *Too much time behind the wheel.* Thankfully, the weather had been mostly clear, only a few patches of snow flurries along the way. It was the length of the drive that had gotten to him. They'd only stopped long enough to grab something to eat and use the restroom.

Delaney could tell Corbin was getting tired and had offered to drive, but he insisted that he was fine. He wanted to stay behind the wheel in case they had to make a break for it. Luckily, that hadn't been necessary. Sutton's plan appeared to be working like a charm. Sutton called a couple of hours ago, telling them that Hugh had taken the bait and was on his way to Northern Cal. Sutton had even gone so far as to get a double to pose as Delaney in a heavily-guarded safe house. His thoughts went to Anton. Sutton interrogated him, but sadly, Anton knew very little about the inner-workings of Hugh's operation.

Corbin's stomach tightened as they passed his grandmother's care center. He couldn't stand the thought of her being alone in that cold, sterile building. For years, Pops had tried to manage her illness, but Gram kept getting out of the house.

They moved through the downtown district, past the neat rows of Western-style buildings flanking both sides of the road. Birchwood Springs was known for two things—Bear Claw Ski Resort and Birchwood Hot Springs located a quarter mile outside the town district. He smiled thinking how he wouldn't mind getting Delaney all to himself in the hot springs.

He glanced up to where the tall mountain sat in the distance.

There was no more than a hint of a shadow of it in the darkness, but his mind filled in the details. In the daylight, the glistening snow looked like a thick layer of smooth icing poured over the entirety, the base of the mountain hugging Birchwood Springs like a mother embracing her child.

Coming home always evoked conflicting emotions. Corbin was fond of this place and yet, he'd been so angry as a youth that he was often in trouble with the law for silly things—soaping up the fountain in front of the bank, driving too fast, sneaking into the ski resort without paying. Sheriff Cliff Hendricks would agree wholeheartedly with Delaney describing Corbin as a menace. The sheriff had always hated him like he had some personal vendetta to make sure Corbin always stayed at the bottom. Corbin felt like Birchwood Springs was the best place to keep Delaney safe, otherwise he wouldn't have come.

Ten minutes later, Corbin pulled into the driveway of Pops' cabin, the place where Corbin grew up. The property consisted of a dozen get-away cabins Pops rented to tourists who visited the ski resort and hot springs. Pops lived in one of them year-round. Even during what was considered "peak season" Birchwood Springs was a sleepy little town. It was even more secluded here on Pops' property, making it an ideal place to bring Delaney.

Delaney sat up in her seat and rubbed her eyes. "Sorry I fell asleep." She suppressed a yawn.

"I'm glad you got some rest."

She looked around, trying to come fully awake. "Where are we?"

"Birchwood Springs ... my grandfather's cabins, to be exact. We'll go in. I'll introduce you to him and my sister. We'll grab a key to the cabin where we'll be staying." He grinned. "Remember, we're a couple, so pretend you like me." He wasn't about to tell her that Pops knew the truth.

She rolled her eyes, her voice going extra twangy. "Yeah, yeah. I got it. Don't worry. I'll put on a convincing performance, sugar."

"All right, sweet cheeks, let's do it." He could hardly say the words without laughing, especially when he saw the horrified look on her face.

"Sweet cheeks? Seriously? That's a little over the top."

He pursed his lips. "You're right. Too much. *Babe*. How about that?"

She sighed. "I guess *babe* will have to do."

"Don't touch that door," he said when she reached for the handle.

"Huh? Wariness swept into her eyes. I thought you said no one followed us."

"We're safe. It's not that. My woman would never open her own door."

She blinked a couple of times. "Oh. But it's just us."

"You never know who could be watching. We can't let our guard down." As if on cue, the curtain moved and Addie looked out.

He motioned. "See. I rest my case."

"Thanks." She tilted her head, looking thoughtful. "You sure you're not from the South?"

He chuckled. "Yeah, why?"

"I thought only Southern men opened doors for women. You know, the gentleman thing."

"I've got news for ya, Dee." He spoke her name like a caress, peering into her eyes. "Southern men don't have the monopoly on chivalry."

She rewarded him with a genuine smile, the lines around her eyes crinkling. "That's good to know," she said softly.

A charge of energy raced through his veins as he leaned closer. "Should we kiss and give my sister something to talk about?"

Delaney's eyes rounded as she drew back. "What?"

He placed a hand on her arm. "Addie's still at the window, watching." He didn't know if she was or not, but it sounded plausible. "If we kiss now, it'll be old hat when we kiss in front of people." He caught the flicker of desire in her eyes, knew she wanted this as much as he. Her breath hitched when he touched her cheek. "Just one little kiss," he murmured, trailing his finger along the line of her jaw. "For practice sake." He memorized her features, thinking he'd never seen a more exquisite woman. Her long lashes, the dainty upward tilt of her nose, her full lips. Something shifted in her eyes, then her lips parted in acceptance. A zing shot through him as his mouth touched hers. *Go slow*, his mind commanded. The kiss was deliciously sweet, her lips soft and accepting. How easy it would've been to gather her in his arms, crush her lips with his until neither of them could breathe. Somehow, he managed to gather the strength to pull away. He scoped her face, trying to discern the expression in her dark eyes. Surely, she had to have felt the river of fire that flowed between them. "That wasn't so bad, was it?" He kept his voice casual, even though the question meant so much more.

"Not bad."

Crash and burn. "Ouch."

She laughed lightly. "Not bad for a menace," she winked.

She'd turned the tables ... was teasing him. He couldn't stop a broad grin from filling his face. "I guess I deserved that." She certainly knew how to dish it out. He liked her more each passing second. He motioned with his head. "You ready to go in?"

"Let's do it, sweet cheeks."

He winced. "Ugh! I should've never started that. If Addie hears you call me that, there'll be no end to her teasing."

She laughed. "Any girl who can put you in your place has to be worth her salt."

"Ha! Now that hurts." He opened the door and rushed around to get her door. He opened it with a slight bow. "After you, babe."

She stepped out, pushing her purse strap over her shoulder. "Thanks, hon." She winked, her voice going sugary sweet.

He punched the clicker to lock the doors as she slid an arm through his, pulling him close. "I can't wait to meet your family," she gushed.

Delaney was performing. Corbin looked sideways at her, recognizing the same expression on her face that she'd worn at the senator's birthday party. She'd started performing right after their kiss to protect herself from any real feelings. Disappointment settled over him. He wanted the real version of Delaney, not the pretend one. Yet, this whole boyfriend/girlfriend thing was pretense, so he couldn't fault her for playing her part. He'd just told her to pretend. "Better tone it down a notch," he warned as they got to the door. "Addie'll see right through you. Just be yourself."

She nodded, her lips forming a grim line. "Okay."

He knocked once before opening it. "Hello," he announced. "We're here."

12

The first time Delaney ever performed in front of an audience, she'd been shaking in her boots to the point where she could barely hold a microphone. Tonight, walking through the door of Corbin's grandfather's home, she felt the same way. That kiss had thrown her for a loop. It had been every bit as good as the one in her dream. Well, except for Corbin holding back like she was a China doll that could break if he touched her too hard. She'd wanted more ... wanted to lose herself in his lips ... wanted to satisfy this incredible longing building inside her. Was she losing her mind? She was pushing Corbin away with one hand and pulling him toward her with the other. He probably thought she was the biggest tease. That wasn't her intent at all, however. She was just trying to figure all of this out.

She leaned into Corbin for support, glad to have his arm around her as they went into the living room. Addie was the first to approach. Delaney instantly saw the resemblance. Same color eyes with the same intelligent light in them, same stubborn set of the chin. But Addie's features were softer. Her dark hair fell past her shoulders in tight corkscrew curls. She was thin and tall, standing a good four inches above Delaney.

Corbin let go of Delaney and hugged his sister.

"Hey, Bro. Great to see you. I was beginning to think you'd never come back home."

She stepped back and looked at Delaney. "And you brought a girl with you." Her eyes danced as she clucked her tongue. "Wonders never cease."

Delaney thrust out her hand to shake, but Addie just looked at it and chuckled. "No shakes in this family. Only hugs." She pulled Delaney into a tight embrace. Delaney caught a whiff of Addie's fruity shampoo and fought the urge to touch her wig. Hopefully, it wouldn't fall off. The thought sent a burst of heat across her forehead, making it go moist. She'd not thought about that. What if she was out somewhere and the wig fell off?

Addie looked her up and down. "You're very pretty."

"Thanks." Delaney looked past Addie to Corbin's grandfather. He was Corbin's height with a shock of silver hair and golden, wrinkly skin that suggested a lifetime spent in the sun. She offered a tentative smile. "Hello."

"Hello. I'm Wallace. It's a pleasure to have you in our home." He returned her smile with a genuine one of his own, revealing neat rows of white teeth. It hit her. Corbin and his grandfather had the same smile. "Welcome to Birchwood Springs," he said heartily, embracing Delaney in a tight hug.

Delaney decided right there and then that she liked Wallace Spencer. He'd only just met her, yet welcomed her with such genuineness. If she had a grandfather in her life, she'd want him to be like Wallace. Aside from their smiles and height, Corbin and his grandfather didn't look that much alike. But there was something similar about them. She tried to pinpoint what it was. Maybe it was the fearless look in their eyes. Yes, could be. Although Wallace seemed tamer like he had a longer fuse, a fine wine that had aged gracefully.

Wallace turned his attention to Corbin. The two searched one another's faces, some sort of silent information passing between them. "I'm glad you came home, son." He hugged Corbin and patted his shoulder. Then he motioned. "Have a seat."

Delaney followed Corbin to the love seat where they sat down. He draped an arm around her as if it were the most casual thing in the world. She ignored the attraction that buzzed through her.

Wallace and Addie sat down on the couch across from them.

"How was the drive?" Wallace began, looking from Corbin to Delaney.

"Not too bad," Corbin said.

"Did you come in from Denver?" Addie asked.

Delaney tensed, hating the subterfuge. She glanced at Corbin, whose expression never changed. "Yes."

"I love your Southern accent," Addie said. "Where are you from?"

"Alabama." Corbin had instructed her to tell as much of the truth as she could. That way, they'd have less chance of getting tripped up.

Addie's eyes sparked interest as she tucked a curl behind her ear and leaned forward. "So, how did you two meet?"

A giggle rumbled in Delaney's throat as she looked at Corbin who had a quirky grin on his handsome face. Yep, she'd known that question would be at the top of the list.

"Should I tell her? Or do you want to?" Corbin asked.

Crap. They'd started talking about their cover story then got side-tracked by their disagreement. "We met at a party," she began. Corbin sniggered, and she couldn't help but laugh.

"I don't get it. What's so funny?" Addie frowned, looking from one to the other.

"An inside joke," Corbin said.

Addie harrumphed. "You and your inside jokes." She looked at Delaney. "You'll get used to those."

"Oh, I already have," Delaney agreed. "And you're right. They can be annoying." This won her a look of approval from Addie.

"I knew I liked you," Addie chuckled, tucking her leg underneath her.

Corbin groaned giving Wallace a pleading look. "Now the two of them are ganging up on me."

Wallace spread his hands, smiling. "That's how it works. Better get used to it."

Delaney laughed. "I'm sure you can handle it." She turned to Corbin patting his cheek. "Right, sweet cheeks?"

"Sweet cheeks?" Addie howled with laughter.

Wallace's eyes went large. He tried to hold back a laugh but it came out in a burst that gave way to a string of muffled chortles, his shoulders shaking. He held up a hand, giving Corbin an apologetic look. "Sorry, I shouldn't laugh, but that's funny."

Color blotched up Corbin's neck, his eyes shooting daggers at Delaney. She just laughed and winked at him, loving putting him on the spot for once instead of the other way around.

"Ooh, she's good," Addie cooed. "Keeps you on your toes, bro. Better hold onto her."

Corbin pulled her closer. "Oh, don't worry. I intend to."

The sure promise in his voice reverberated through Delaney like the hum of an ocean current ... steady, permanent, and all-consuming.

"Okay," Addie said impatiently. "Tell me the story."

Delaney's brain raced to come up with something sensible. Corbin worked at a bar in Denver before taking on her assignment, meaning it would be logical that they would've met there. She turned to Corbin, whose eyes were sparking amusement. Was he really going to sit there and let her flounder? *Help me*, she pled silently.

Corbin grabbed her free hand, linking his fingers through hers. Her pulse cranked up a notch. When he started rubbing circles over her thumb, her heartbeat shot through the roof. How in the heck was she supposed to concentrate on the conversation with Corbin touching her this way? "Like Dee said, we met at a party," Corbin said with a straight face. "She teaches music at a middle school. Dee hosted a party for her kids, a reward for their performance. I was working security for the school during special events." He flashed Delaney a very convincing affectionate smile as he squeezed her shoulders. "I looked at her, she looked at me. The rest is history. Right, babe?"

Delaney forced a smile. "Right." Dang. Corbin was good. She could almost believe the story herself. She didn't know if she should be impressed or concerned at how smoothly the fabrications flowed from his lips. Another reason why she needed to be leery of him. How could she ever be sure that the man she was seeing was the real deal?

Addie untucked her leg, shifting to get comfortable. "So, you teach middle school kids? I'll bet that's a challenge."

"You have no idea," Delaney said, causing everyone to laugh.

"What do you have planned during your stay here?" Addie asked.

Delaney looked to Corbin to answer that. Addie seemed nice enough, but the barrage of questions was getting a little tiresome, especially after the long drive.

As if reading Delaney's thoughts, Wallace touched Addie's arm. "There'll be plenty of time to talk later, after Corbin and Dee have had a chance to rest."

"Rest?" Addie wrinkled her nose. "They only had a two-and-a-half-hour drive."

Delaney fought the urge to roll her eyes. *If only.*

"Yeah, sis. You're right. But Delaney had to get up early this morning to teach her class before we could head out of town, and I had a late night at work the night before." He yawned. "Like Pops said, we're worn out."

Addie cocked her head like she'd just thought of something. "Who's watching your classes while you're here?"

Geez! The firestorm of questions was getting old. Delaney fought to keep her voice pleasant. "I got a sub." She smiled adoringly at Corbin. "As much as I hated to leave my students, I wanted to come here and meet Corbin's family, see where he grew up."

Addie's eyes sparkled. "You should go to the sweetheart dance this weekend at the ski resort." She wiggled her eyebrows at Corbin. "Show Dee off." A wicked grin curved her lips. "Madison Wells will be green with envy. She was asking about you the other day."

Sweetheart dance? Certainly not something Delaney wanted to attend under the circumstance. She felt Corbin tense, realized he was looking at Addie like he wanted to stuff a sock in her mouth. "Who's Madison Wells?" she asked before she could stop herself.

"Nobody," Corbin muttered.

Addie laughed. "His ex-girlfriend. They broke up before Corbin joined the Navy, but Madison's still got a thing for him."

The stab of jealousy that went through Delaney came as a surprise. Then she had to laugh at herself. Why did she care who Corbin's ex-girlfriend was? She realized Addie was watching, waiting for her reaction. Let's see ... how would a real girlfriend react? She arched an eyebrow, putting on a touch of a wounded expression mingled with frustration as she looked at Corbin. "You never mentioned Madison."

It was fun watching Corbin squirm. "That's because it was over a long time ago." He shot Addie a frustrated look. "Ancient history. I assure you, there've been plenty of other girls since Madison Wells."

"Really?" Delaney arched an eyebrow. "That's good to know." This time, her irritation was real.

Wallace stood, shaking his head. "All right, Addie. That's enough grilling for one night."

Addie thrust out her lower lip, smirking at Corbin. "I was just getting started."

"Yeah, that's what I'm afraid of," Corbin said dryly. "Little sis has been sharpening her knives."

"Only because you never come home," Addie retorted.

This was the second time Addie mentioned that. Delaney made a mental note to ask Corbin why he didn't want to come home. Wallace seemed great. And yeah, Addie was a little annoying, but it was obvious she was just needling Corbin so he'd pay attention to her. Even through the teasing, Delaney could tell Addie adored her brother.

Corbin and Delaney stood. Hesitantly, Addie did the same.

"I'll go and get the keys. You're staying in cabin eight." Wallace shuffled out of the room.

"You're staying by yourselves in a cabin?" Addie tsked her tongue. "What will people think?"

"I don't really care," Corbin said, his brows bunching.

Addie made a face, zeroing in on Delaney. "How do you put up with his foul moods?"

"It can be tough," Delaney said, not cracking a smile.

Addie laughed. "Like I said, I like her."

Corbin shook his head, his tone mellowing. "It's good to see you, Addie. I've missed you."

For an instant, Addie's eyes went moist, then she blinked to clear them. "You know where I've been, big brother. You could've come home anytime."

He nodded, his lips forming a grim line.

Addie gave him a hard look. "Are you gonna visit Gram while you're here? You haven't been to see her once since she moved to the home."

Delaney looked at Corbin, saw the tension building inside him, felt she had to do something to relieve it. She put a hand on his arm, but he seemed oblivious. He glared at Addie, his face turning a shade darker. "She didn't move to the home, she was put there." The vehemence in his voice took Delaney off guard. But it didn't quell Addie in the slightest.

Addie locked eyes with him. "You need to go and visit her."

Corbin's jaw tightened. "Why? She won't even know I'm there."

The hurt in his voice struck something deep inside Delaney, bringing tears to her eyes.

Wallace came back into the room. He stopped, concern washing over him. "Is everything okay?"

"As good as it ever is." Addie waved a hand. "I'm going to bed. Goodnight, folks." She turned on her heel and strode out.

"What was that all about?" Wallace stepped up to Corbin and placed the keys in his hand.

"Nothing," Corbin grumbled.

Wallace looked at Delaney like he wanted her to explain, but she only shook her head and smiled politely. She had enough problems of her own without getting in the middle of this family's.

"I'm really glad you came," Wallace said to Corbin. "It's the best place to keep her safe."

Delaney's jaw went slack as she turned to Corbin. "He knows?"

"Yes, I called Pops last night and explained the situation. I wanted to make sure it was okay if I brought you here. If Hugh were to find us, it could potentially put my family at risk. I wanted Pops to have all the information before he agreed."

A shiver went down Delaney's spine. She couldn't stand the thought of Hugh doing anything to Corbin's family. "I hadn't thought about that. I don't want to put your family in danger." Tears pressed against her eyes, panic building inside her. "We have to go someplace else." Her mind whirled trying to figure out where that place was. Maybe Anton was right. No place was beyond Hugh's reach.

Corbin took hold of her arm. "No, this is the best place to keep you safe. The plan is set. We just have to follow it and trust that Sutton's taking care of everything on his end."

"He's right," Wallace said. "You'll be safe here. Corbin knows this place like the back of his hand. I'm glad he brought you."

She searched the man's lined face touched by the wisdom of having lived a long, productive life. "Are you sure?"

He smiled. "Absolutely." His gravelly tone held all the confidence in the world, the voice of reason amid chaos. "What you both need right now is a good night's rest. Things will look brighter in the morning. I picked up a few things from the store today. You'll find them in the fridge and on the counter." He gave Delaney a reassuring look. "It'll be all right."

A tear rolled down her cheek. She wasn't used to people being this kind. "Thank you."

Wallace gave her a nod of acknowledgement.

She thought of something else. "What about Addie? Does she know the truth?"

Corbin spoke up. "No. It's better to keep Addie in the dark, for her own safety. Pops is the only one who knows."

"I'll come around mid-morning to check on you," Wallace said.

Appreciation flashed in Corbin's eyes. "Thanks, Pops."

"Sure thing." Wallace gave Corbin a hearty pat on the shoulder. "Goodnight."

"Goodnight," Delaney said as they went out the door into the frosty night air. A hundred large snowflakes pinged her face all at once. There hadn't been a single snowflake in the air when they'd gone into the cabin and now, during the short time they were inside, it was coming a blizzard. All she could see were endless streaks of white against the black velvet darkness. She hugged her arms, chills racing through her. It was sunny and warm when they left San Diego this morning. And now this. Everything was happening so fast, she could hardly wrap her mind around it. When Corbin put an arm around her, she snuggled into the warmth of his shoulder as they walked, heads down to the SUV.

"Let's get you to the cabin where it's warm," Corbin said, opening her door and helping her inside.

Regardless of the conflicting feelings she had for Corbin, she was grateful that he was here with her ... keeping her safe.

13

The wheels spun a little, trying to gain traction until Corbin popped it into 4-wheel drive and maneuvered the SUV up the hill and around the bend to the cabin. He was grateful that the roads were clear earlier. If a storm had to hit at least it was after they'd arrived. The snow pounding against the windshield reminded him of a meteor shower. The windshield wipers were of little help. The instant they brushed the flakes away, thousands more took their places.

"Can you even see?" Delaney was leaning forward in her seat, her voice strained.

"Yeah, we'll be fine," he answered, even though he really couldn't see very well. "The cabin's just up here." He could feel Delaney's relief when they pulled into the driveway.

"Let's get you inside, and I'll come back for the luggage."

"Thanks." Delaney shivered, giving him a slight smile. "I guess you were right. I should've worn the thicker coat instead of leaving it in the suitcase."

When they set out this morning, Corbin questioned Delaney's choice of clothing, reminding her that Colorado winters were nothing like the mild ones in San Diego. Delaney brushed aside the comment saying she'd be fine. He couldn't help but smile a little inwardly. At least she didn't mind admitting that she'd been wrong. "The good news is that you have lots of winter clothes in your suitcase."

"Yeah, I'm glad Sutton thought of it."

"Me too." Birchwood Springs only had a handful of shops with a scanty selection of clothing. It was nice that they wouldn't have to worry about it. The wind pushed against the driver door, making it hard to open. He tucked his chin into his neck as he went around to get Delaney's door. Cabin eight was near the back of the property in one of the more secluded spots. Pops had chosen it for added privacy. Snow was accumulating fast, already a good six inches on the ground. Delaney got out, leaning into him for cover as they made their way to the door. Even though he knew she was only getting this close to him because he was shielding her from the snow, it felt good to be next to her.

He'd wondered how Delaney would react to his family. She seemed to do just fine, despite Addie's intrusiveness. It felt so natural to sit in Pops' living room, his arm around Delaney as they talked. They trudged up the steps to the door where Corbin shoved in the key, turned the lock, and pushed open the door. The two of them practically fell into the shelter of the cabin as they brushed off the snow. Corbin flipped on the lights and looked around.

It was the same as he remembered—exposed rough timber beams on the ceiling, log walls, a wooden staircase leading up to the bedrooms on the second floor, woodsy furnishings. An open floor plan included the living room and kitchen in one big area. He looked at the efficiency kitchen. A kettle was on the stovetop, a dishtowel draped over the oven door. His gaze moved back to the living room, his eyes resting on the emerald afghan draped over the back of the couch—Gram's handiwork. His heart clutched as memories gushed over him. One autumn, Gram decided to crochet afghans for all the cabins to give them a homey feel. What she thought would take three months took seven, but she completed her goal.

Standing here in this cabin with a floor plan identical to all the others, Corbin got a sense of the years peeling away, almost like he'd never left. Despite the sadness of Gram's situation, there was a certain comfort from the familiarity. Like Pops said, he knew this place like the back of his hand, and would be able to keep Delaney safe here. He breathed in the familiar scent of lemon cleaning solution mingled with cedar. Hilda Bryant had been cleaning the cabins for years, ever since Corbin was a boy. She loved lemon. "I'll be right back. Make yourself at home."

Delaney took off her shoes, then went to the tweed sofa and deposited her purse. She stood, looking around like she was unsure what to do. Corbin understood her hesitation. This was a far cry from San Diego, that was for sure. She rubbed her arms like she was cold.

"I'll start a fire as soon as I get everything in." Pops kept a large supply of seasoned firewood in a covered box beside the front door, along with an axe and chopping block. While there was no central heat, there was a fireplace in the living room and pot belly stove in the kitchen. The bedrooms had portable heaters. When a fire was going, the cabin was cozy and romantic. Although, Delaney would balk if he dared bring up the latter.

Once the luggage was in, he locked the door and clicked the dead-bolt. Tomorrow, he'd do a thorough check of the perimeter to make sure everything was secure. It was good to know that Hugh and his goons had taken the bait and were far away in Northern Cal. Delaney was sitting on the couch, the TV on. There were only a handful of channels available, mostly local stations. She was watching the news. She glanced at the luggage. "Do you need any help?"

"Sure."

She stood and reached for her guitar. "Which room am I staying in?"

It was a two-bedroom, two bath. "I'll let you take the master, and I'll sleep in the guest room next door."

"Are you sure?"

"Absolutely."

A smile touched her lips.

"What?"

"You sound just like your grandfather. He seems like such a nice man."

He frowned. "He's okay."

She looked puzzled. "You don't like him?"

"Of course I like him. He's my grandfather, practically my father." The last thing Corbin wanted to go into was his complex relationship with Pops. While Pops had mellowed in his older years, he'd been hard as nails when Corbin was growing up, expecting nothing less than perfection. Pops didn't like Corbin questioning his authority, which he did on a regular basis. Gram had been the buffer between them. When she got sick, the situation escalated with the heightened emotions, making things between him and Pops intolerable.

Corbin couldn't stand watching Gram wither away, so he joined the Navy. Addie accused him of using it as an escape. Maybe he had. But the Navy and then later the SEALs gave him purpose, a way to channel his anger. It had worked well until Doug was killed and everything fell apart. Doug had been his rock, his compass. Had it not been for Doug, Corbin never would've made it through BUD/S training, and especially not Hell Week, that five and a half day stretch where they were forced to operate on four hours of sleep. Men were dropping like flies—men who seemed a lot tougher than Corbin. There were many days when Corbin had been ready to ring the brass bell to tap out, but Doug's response was always the same. "You can ring it tomorrow if you want, but not today. Today we conquer." In BUD/S training, conquering meant surviving the day.

Corbin hauled the heavy suitcase up the steps. Delaney was in front, carrying her guitar and a duffel bag. At the top, he motioned. "The master's this way." Corbin placed Delaney's suitcase on the floor beside her bed. A smile slid over his lips as he gave her an offhanded look. "What's in here? Rocks?"

She shrugged. "Hey, don't blame me. I didn't order all that stuff."

"True," he conceded. "Are you normally a heavy or light packer?"

She leaned her guitar against the wall, dropped the duffle bag on the floor, then plopped down on the bed. "Is this one of those times when anything I say can and will be used against me?"

He laughed, liking that she was bantering with him, even though they were both weary to the bone. "Maybe."

"I'm Southern. And Southern girls never do anything small." She stretched out her legs, leaning back against the headboard. "I'm so exhausted." She yawned as she spoke.

"Me too," Corbin agreed. His mind ran through the set-up of the cabin. "The bathroom is a Jack and Jill style, shared between our bedrooms."

Her face fell. "Oh."

"If it bothers you, I can use the one downstairs."

"I hate for you to do that. We can share."

He searched her face. "Are you sure?"

"Absolutely." She said it like Pops, breaking the word into pronounced syllables. They both smiled, sharing the moment.

She reached up and pulled off her wig and placed it on the nearby nightstand. Then she removed the hair net, her blonde locks falling over her shoulders. "I'm so glad to have that thing off my head. My scalp's itching like crazy." She scratched her head, then ran her hands through her roots, fluffing it up. Corbin's breath caught thinking of how it would feel to run his fingers through her hair. She looked like an angel, the most intoxicating woman he'd ever seen. She tipped her head, a smile tugging at her lips. "What?"

"You're beautiful," he said softly. He thought about their kiss and how it had consumed him, making him want more. Next time he wanted to kiss her the right way, holding nothing back. Briefly, he wondered how she would react if he went to her this instant and pulled her into his arms. Her swift reaction to his compliment was his answer.

Her eyes widened, and she looked like she wanted to retreat. "Thanks."

"Sorry, I don't mean to make you uncomfortable. I have a terrible habit of speaking before I think."

She relaxed a little. "No worries." She paused, looking thoughtful. "It was nice getting to know your family."

"They really like you."

"Really? I wasn't sure what Addie thought of me." She wrinkled her nose. "Is she always so inquisitive?"

He chuckled. "Yeah, she's the nosiest woman on the planet. She likes to pretend like she's tough, but inside, she's a teddy bear."

Corbin felt a little foolish standing in the middle of the room. Did he dare sit down on the edge of the bed? There weren't any chairs. No, he'd better not chance it. Delaney might freak out. It felt intimate enough with the two of them alone in this cabin, then add that he was standing in her bedroom. Better keep a respectable distance.

"Thanks for everything. If you don't mind, I think I'll turn in for the night."

That was his cue to leave. "You sure you don't want me to start a fire? I could make us some hot chocolate. That's one of Pops' staples, I'm sure he bought some."

A wistful look touched her features, giving him hope that she might accept his invitation, but the expression vanished as quickly as it had come. "I'm really tired."

He sighed. "All right. If you need anything, let me know." He jutted his thumb. "I'll be right next door. When you're in the bathroom, just keep the door to my room closed and locked, and I'll know not to go in."

She nodded.

"Oh, and feel free to turn on the heater so you don't freeze to death." He grinned a little at the sight of her, hugging her arms like it was twelve below zero in the room. He was used to the cold, even enjoyed it most of the time. But Delaney was used to the mild San Diego weather. Funny how he'd thought he wanted to use his newfound income to go somewhere warm and now he was kind of glad to be snowed in with Delaney. "Here, I'll do it for you."

"Thanks."

After the heater was plugged in, he turned to leave, then stopped, turning to face her. He couldn't stop the goofy grin from spilling over his lips. "By the way, you did good tonight ... pretending to be my girlfriend."

She blinked in surprise as a deep blush brushed her cheekbones, making her look even more incredible. She smiled hesitantly. "You didn't do so bad yourself, Captain America."

The compliment sent warm bubbles bursting through him. It took all the fortitude he could muster not to close the distance between them and pull her into his arms. His eyes held hers. "I guess we fit together better than we thought, huh?"

She flinched, hugging her arms even tighter. "Goodnight," she clipped.

"Goodnight," he repeated dully. *One step forward, ten steps back.* At this rate, he'd be sixty before he won her over.

CORBIN WAS EXHAUSTED and yet too keyed up to sleep. The wind howled like a lonely wolf outside his window, making him glad he was inside, snuggled under the heavy blanket. It was crazy to think how quickly his life had changed. One minute he was working a dead-end job and the next he was on a plane to San Diego. Now, he was back home, the most fascinating woman he'd ever met sleeping next door.

Of course all was not fun and games. He had to keep Delaney safe from a ruthless killer. Goosebumps prickled over his flesh as he looked at the Glock on the nightstand. He'd kept it nearby, just in case. Before turning in for the night, he'd called Sutton and reported in. That was their system—he'd call in every night on a secure line letting Sutton know the status. Sutton asked if Corbin needed any backup. He told Sutton that as long as Hugh was in Northern Cal, he was fine on his own. But that could change in a heartbeat.

He closed his eyes, willing his mind to shut down for the night. An image of Delaney flashed before his mind. Their kiss had not been acting, he was sure of it. They'd probably need to stay in the cabin, keep away from people as much as possible. But Corbin hoped they might be able to get out a little. He'd love to take Delaney on a snowmobile ride or to the hot springs. If they went at night, there would be fewer people. He'd pull her close, let his fingers get lost in her magnificent hair. Feel her soft lips against his.

Finally, he felt himself drift off to sleep.

THIS IS A DREAM, Corbin told himself. And yet it felt so real. The memories came as they always did, like fragments of splintered glass that shifted at random to create distorted pictures of reality. He felt the camaraderie of SEAL Team 7—a band of brothers whose allegiance to country was only equaled by their loyalty to each other. Never had Corbin felt so much acceptance from a group.

Their orders were clear—rescue a diplomat and his family held hostage by a terrorist cell in a remote village.

The fragments shifted. Heat crowded out all else. A heat so oppressive that it was like being trapped in a wet oven, basting in your own sweat. The lightweight vest was designed for jungle ops and yet, it still felt heavy against Corbin's chest. He wished he could rip the wretched thing off, give his skin a chance to cool off. He could've been stark naked and still be sweltering. And it was the middle of the night! Insane that it would still be so hot!

They walked like phantoms through the thick vegetation of the Filipino jungle, trying to stay clear of the slithery creatures that ravaged nearly every square inch of the moist, tangled landscape. A faint taste of spice lingered in the night air. His boots made a soft sucking sound against the thick mud. To Corbin's ears, his steps were as loud as firecrackers, but he knew his senses were exaggerated. Their footsteps would be masked by the rhythmic shrieks and cries from tree frogs and a million other jungle creatures. Doug was on Corbin's right. By common consent, the two of them never ventured far from one another's sides. Before they'd gone quiet, Doug teased him about the need to find a good woman and settle down. Corbin had laughed. "I'll leave that to you, buddy."

The scene changed. They were inside the village. From all appearances, the inhabitants were deep in a peaceful slumber. Stealthily, they made their way toward the two-story structure where the family was being held, at least according to intel. The information had come from a trusted source, but there was always a chance of it being erroneous.

Zane, the Commanding Officer, held up a hand for them to halt as he assessed the situation. Corbin clutched his assault rifle, his eyes scanning through the darkness, looking for any signs of movement. Finally, after what seemed like an eternity, Zane waved the group forward.

They were about twenty yards from entering the house when everything broke loose. Shadows rushing at them, shots popping like hot grease in a pan. *Ambush!* Corbin's mind screamed.

"Fall back!" Zane ordered, but there was no time. They were caught like fish in a bowl.

A firestorm of bullets rained down. Cover was too far back. Nothing they could do to escape.

Doug rushed forward into the chaos as shots ricocheted in every direction. He tossed a grenade at the delivery truck parked in front of the building. It hit the gas tank on the side, exploding into a ball of flames and shielding the SEALs from the bullets of the enemy.

For a moment, the gunshots stopped. Doug ran back. Corbin waited for him while the other SEALs darted to the cover of a low wall.

"That was gutsy, man!" Corbin exclaimed. "The perfect diversion to get us out of here."

Doug went down, face in the dirt. At first, Corbin thought he'd tripped, then realized with horror that he'd been shot multiple times. Corbin fell to his knees, his tears mixing with the sweat. Corbin ripped off Doug's helmet, the vacant look in his best friend's eyes shredding him to pieces. "No!" he cried.

Cannon took his arm, tried to pull him to his feet, urging him to fall back with the team. But rage boiled through Corbin's veins, crowding out all reason. All he could think about was retribution—a dozen lives for the life of his friend.

His mind shifted to the next events. More commotion. Screams.

Zane's voice coming through the headset. "Stand down!" he yelled. "Abort!" But the command fell on deaf ears. Out of the corner of his eye, Corbin saw the family, huddled together, two men dressed in black carrying semi-automatic rifles—one in front and one in back, leading the family out a side door into the jungle. A mother and father, two young girls, their muffled sobs carrying in the night air.

Corbin began systematically firing at the terrorists, instinct taking over. He dropped the two gunmen in front and back of the family. Then took out several more on the roof.

"You're putting the team and family at risk! Abort!" Zane ordered.

But Corbin's rage knew no limits. He'd get them all! He stepped into the open, no longer caring about his own life as he ignored the shots being fired at him. The next events were seared into his soul. The family running. A terrorist firing at them, the bullet hitting the young girl as she crumpled, blood spilling over her white nightgown. The blood pooled and ran like a river onto the ground. He felt the girl's terror, heard the mother's gut-wrenching cry as she fell to her knees beside the girl. The father trying to drag the mother away.

His grandmother's face took the place of the girl's. Gram had been so good to him, had understood him in a way no one else had. And now, she was alone. Gram was standing at the head of a tunnel. He had to get to her, but his legs were cement, darkness closing in around him.

"Help her!" Corbin cried. A sob broke loose in his throat. "Please!"

14

A cold sweat broke over the bridge of Delaney's nose as she shot up in bed, her hands gripping the covers. Her body trembled as she looked wildly around the dark room, her mind trying to process what was happening. Was Hugh here? An icy terror clutched her.

She heard the deep rumble of Corbin's cry. "Help her! Please!"

Somehow, she managed to find her voice. "Corbin? Are you okay?"

No answer.

For a moment, she wasn't sure what to do. She looked at the closed bedroom door, expecting it to burst open any minute. Nothing.

She heard more muffled cries. Sobbing?

A prayer for help sounded in her mind as she sat there, shaking. Finally, she pushed back the covers and got out of bed. Her heart in her throat, she rushed through the bathroom into Corbin's room. A heady relief covered her, making her go weak in the knees when she realized what was happening. Corbin was having a nightmare.

She stood there, trying to figure out what to do. The tough guy was crying like a baby in his sleep. Compassion washed over her as she went to his bedside. Holding her breath, she touched his shoulder.

"Corbin?"

As he sat up and reached for his gun, she jumped back with a yelp. Terror seized her as she held up her hands. "Don't shoot. It's me!"

Corbin shook his head in a daze, trying to focus on her. Then he put the gun down. He sat back, rubbing his eyes. "I'm sorry," he mumbled so low that she wondered if she'd imagined it.

"You were crying." The cold of the wood floor seeped through her bare feet, spreading ice up her limbs.

She heard a gulp, realized he was still crying ... or at least trying to squelch it. She stepped closer. "Are you okay?"

"It was my fault." The words came out ragged and hoarse.

"What?"

Long pause. And then another choking sound. "The girl's death. If I hadn't gone berserk and started shooting, she'd still be alive today."

A thousand questions pummeled her mind, ending with, *What girl?*

He drew in a halting breath, letting out an embarrassed chuckle as he scooted to sit up. "Sorry, I was still half asleep. Scratch those statements." He ran both hands through his messy hair. "Sorry ... you probably think I'm a head case." He wiped at his tears.

There were two things Delaney was well acquainted with—sorrow and regret. She'd never fault anyone for going through hardships. In fact, she was surprised Tuck's death wasn't plaguing her in her sleep. Her mother's death did often enough. A sliver of moonlight shone in through the window, reflecting off Corbin's strong jaw. Even Captain America had weaknesses. She got a good look at Corbin. Realized with a jolt that he was shirtless. A blast of heat went through her as she looked at his defined pecs and six pack. *Okay, focus on his face*, her mind commanded.

"I'm all right. Just a stupid nightmare," he grumbled.

She clutched her nightgown, knowing how ridiculous she looked in the striped pink and blue gown. She never would've bought this for herself in a million years. She'd considered sleeping in her underwear. But that seemed inappropriate considering Corbin was right next door.

He sighed. "I'm okay now. You can go back to bed."

But he wasn't okay. She could feel his pain, filling the empty space between them. She wanted to know about the girl who'd been killed ... had a right to know. After all, Corbin was the only thing standing between her and a certain death. She needed to know what had happened to him.

She motioned. "Do you care if I sit down?"

"Sure," he said in surprise.

In the full light of day, Delaney was sure she could come up with a thousand reasons why being here in Corbin's bedroom wasn't a good idea. But at this moment, her guard was down. And Corbin needed to talk this out. She didn't know how she was so tuned into a man she hardly knew, but like it or not, that was the case.

She sat down, hugging her arms. It was frigid in here. "Did you not plug in your heater?"

"No, I like it cold when I sleep. Gram used to say that the healthiest way to sleep was to be able to see your breath at night."

"I'm surprised I can't see my breath in here," she said tartly.

He scooted over and patted the spot beside him. "Come here."

Her heart pounded. "I don't think that's a good idea," she squeaked.

"I assure you, I'll be a perfect gentleman. I just don't want you to freeze to death while we talk."

"I could always plug in the heater."

"Yeah, but it'll take at least twenty minutes for the room to heat up."

She spoke through chattering teeth. "I'll be a popsicle by then."

The last of her misgivings slipped away in the wake of his pleading expression. Being here with Corbin ... this was right ... something she didn't need to be afraid of. The thoughts blew across her heart like a tender whisper, sending a blessed cushion of comfort around her.

Corbin motioned with his head to the spot beside him. That's all the encouragement she needed. She hopped over and pulled the covers up over her. True to his word, he scooted to the other side, keeping a healthy distance between them.

She angled to face him. "Okay, tell me about the girl."

THE EXPERIENCE WITH THE SEALs, Doug's death, it wasn't something Corbin liked to talk about. But for some reason, he felt like it would be okay to tell Delaney. Maybe it was the sympathetic look on her face, or the fact that she, too, had suffered pain and loss. Or maybe he simply needed to get the words out, unburden his soul. He cleared his throat attempting to gather his thoughts. "For you to understand, I'll need to tell you from the beginning. When I first became a SEAL."

The memories rushed out like water from a broken dam as Corbin told Delaney about BUD/S training. How it pushed him past any point he ever thought he could go. How Doug had been there by his side, urging him to keep going. He chuckled, remembering. "Unlike me, Doug grew up with a silver spoon in his mouth. As Sutton Smith's only son, the world was his oyster. He had every reason to be full of himself and yet he was the very opposite—the most down-to-earth guy I've ever met."

Delaney sucked in a breath, looking puzzled. "So, your best friend was Sutton's son?"

"Yeah. Doug's the reason I became a SEAL. I would've tapped out early on if it hadn't been for him." He clenched his fist, bitterness coating his throat. "I should've been the one who died, not him." How many times had he wished he could live that horrible night over again? Somehow taking Doug's place. Doug had rushed forward to save everyone while he stayed back. How different things might've been had he gone with Doug to help?

He looked at Delaney, surprised to see tears glistening in her eyes.

She scooted closer and touched his arm, sending electricity surging through him.

"I'm sorry," she said softly. "What happened?"

While Corbin was trying to decide what to tell her and what to hold back, the whole thing gushed out. He told her about the rescue mission, how he'd gone nuts when Doug was killed, started shooting up the place like Rambo. And finally, how he'd been the cause of the girl losing her life. When the words ran dry, he sat there, a guilty man waiting for the jury's verdict.

"You can't keep blaming yourself. You didn't shoot the girl."

A hard laugh escaped his throat. "Can't I? I disobeyed a direct order from my CO. He told me to stand down, that my actions were putting the team and the family at risk. And he was right." The self-loathing rushed back with a vengeance. But it felt good to say the words out loud to another person.

"It was one moment in time. You lost your head ... made a mistake. It could happen to anyone."

He could hardly believe the words coming out of her mouth, thought maybe he'd imagined them because that's what he wanted to hear. "No," he finally said, "I was trained to do better. I should've kept my cool."

"No amount of training could prepare you for losing your best friend. What happened afterwards?"

"The situation was investigated. The ballistics test came back unclear if Doug had been killed by enemy or friendly fire. The government slapped a lid on the incident to prevent a public outcry, and I was transferred to another team. I left the SEALs shortly thereafter." Shame blistered over him, and he could hardly make himself look at Delaney. He forced the words from his dry throat, knowing he had to get them out while he could. "Now that you know what type of man's protecting you, it might be a good idea to call Sutton and request a replacement. I wouldn't blame you if you did." He looked down at his hands, his gut sinking like a lead balloon. It was good that he was being honest with Delaney. Her life was on the line. She deserved to know what kind of man he really was.

"Look at me."

The authority in her voice took him by surprise.

Reluctantly, his eyes met hers, and he was struck by the fierceness of her expression.

She cupped his face, the warmth of her skin flowing into his. "You're a good man. I trust you to keep me safe. You did it once before in the car with Anton, and I know you'll do it again."

Her words burned into his chest, kindling an unexpected hope. "Really?" Tears brimmed in his eyes. He felt like such a fool for crying in front of her and yet the emotion was too much to contain.

"Absolutely."

He chuckled at the reference to Pops. "I can't believe you met my grandfather one time and are already quoting him," he said dryly.

"Well, he seems like a smart guy."

"He's all right, for an old dude," he said offhandedly.

A smile tipped her lips, her dark eyes sparking with a hint of mystery that gave him the feeling that no matter how much time he spent around Delaney, it would never be enough. "So, Corbin Spencer, will you still be my pretend boyfriend?"

He looked down at her ridiculous-looking nightgown, his gaze lingering on the ruffles around her neck. "I dunno," he drawled. "My woman would never wear that."

She laughed. "Yeah, it's pretty bad."

"It's okay for a nineteenth-century farm girl."

Her smile grew larger. "You know, I thought the exact same thing. Did Sutton have this hidden away in some trunk?"

"Maybe it belongs to his assistant Agatha. It looks like something an old lady would wear."

She giggled. "Yes, it does."

Corbin's heart felt lighter than it had in a long time ... longer than he could even remember. He'd bared his soul to Delaney and she was okay with the things he'd done. He still found it hard to believe, but he wasn't about to look a gift horse in the mouth. He leaned in, closing the distance between them. "So," he said huskily, "would it be okay to give my pretend girlfriend another kiss? For practice?"

Delaney's cheeks grew flush, but she didn't retreat. There was a smolder of desire in her eyes that matched the fire igniting in him. "Okay, but only for practice."

He pulled her into his arms, his lips taking hers. She tipped her head back, a groan sounding in her throat as she slid her arms around his shoulders. This time, he didn't hold back. He ran his fingers through her hair, their lips moving together in a burst of energy and flames. He was being consumed by this woman. And it was happening so fast, he could hardly process it.

She pulled back, breathing hard. "I think we've got that move down pretty good."

"I believe you're right." He grinned. "But I'll never say *no* to practice."

Her eyes grew troubled as she looked around like she just now realized what was happening. "I shouldn't be here with you." She shuddered. "I'm not that kind of woman."

Panic raced through him. She was retreating. It was like a switch suddenly flipped in her brain. She moved to escape, but he caught her arm. "Hey, don't do this."

"What?"

"Run ... from us."

She gurgled out a laugh. "There is no *us*. This is pretend—a charade invented to keep me safe."

He let go of her arm and trailed a finger down a tendril of her hair. "This is real." His eyes locked with hers. "You know it." He could tell from her expression that he was right.

"I can't get involved with you right now. Not when we're in the middle of all this."

He held her gaze. "Afterwards?"

She shrugged, giving him a small, sad smile. "Afterwards, we'll see."

He could tell she had no intention of entertaining a relationship with him, and it cut. All the angst rushed back. "Because of what I told you? About my past?" It was stupid to think she could accept him, that anyone could. After what he'd done.

"No. Because of me ... and my past." Her eyes teared up. "I'm damaged goods."

He touched her face. "No, you're an angel ... the most beautiful, intoxicating woman I've ever been around." He could tell from the doubt in her eyes that she didn't believe him. "I wish you could see what I see. You pulled yourself up from nothing. Made something of yourself. You looked fear in the eyes and kept moving forward. All of those things are heroic."

She drew back from him, a tear dribbling down her cheek. Hastily, she brushed it away with her palm. "I need to get some rest ... in my own room."

Maybe they were a lost cause. He was no psychiatrist, couldn't imagine all that Delaney had been through to bring her to this point. He didn't know how to reach her. Every time he felt like he was getting close, she retreated even farther away. A bleak emptiness settled over him as he nodded. "All right. Good night."

She scuttled out of the bed. "Good night," she said over her shoulder, rushing out of the room.

15

For a moment, right after she awoke, Delaney was confused about where she was. Then everything came back in a flash —Tuck's death, Hugh out for revenge, fleeing to the cabin. And last night ... the kiss in Corbin's bed. She sat up, her cheeks burning with remembrance. She couldn't deny that the feelings Corbin stirred in her were stronger than any she'd ever had. Tuck had been her only other relationship and that was so messed up and tainted that she really had nothing to go off of. She scrunched her nose, realizing she'd just dubbed this thing with Corbin a relationship.

Corbin probably thought she was a total moron, kissing him and then fleeing. Right after she told him he was a good man and that she trusted him to keep her safe. She did trust him to keep her safe, but she didn't trust him with her heart. Maybe she'd never be able to trust anyone. Like she said, she was damaged goods.

She got up and looked out the window, struck by the splendor of the landscape. It was a winter wonderland. The rolling hills of pristine snow were surrounded by a hedge of towering evergreen trees. Above that, the crisp blue sky was streaked with wisps of hazy clouds. *Always those clouds in the sky.* At least today, they weren't obscuring the sun. A tingle of excitement ran through her. Not a bad place to spend the next few days writing songs. Then again, they could be here much longer, depending on how this thing with Hugh played out.

The bathroom door was open to Corbin's bedroom. Her pulse picked up a notch as she ran her hand over her nightgown then up to her hair. She didn't want Corbin to see her with bedhead. Then again, it didn't matter how messy her hair was because she was going to wear the wig over it. She looked at the hair on the nightstand, half expecting it to start crawling. It really did look like some sort of animal.

She rummaged through the suitcase, looking for something warm and comfortable to wear. She chose jeans and a red sweater. Thankfully, most of the outerwear clothing was leaps better than the sleepwear.

She walked through the bathroom and stood at the door leading to Corbin's room. Hesitantly, she peeked in. The bed was made, Corbin's duffel bag resting on the floor at the foot of the bed. His laptop was sitting on the dresser. He was probably downstairs waiting for her. What time was it, anyway? Eight or nine a.m.? She missed her phone, missed getting on Instagram and Twitter to chat with her fans. Hopefully, Milo would take up the slack while she was gone.

Supposedly, everything had been worked out with the execs at Montana Crew's label, but what if something fell through the cracks? Anxiety streaked through her. She couldn't afford to make any more mistakes with her career. The negative publicity Tuck's death caused was bad enough. She needed to get these blasted songs written and recorded for the album to stay on task. She'd be going on tour the end of next month and needed to have something for fans to purchase ... something to keep her relevant.

She closed and locked both doors to the bathroom before turning on the shower. A couple of seconds later, she stepped in, letting the hot water run over her shoulders. Her mind went through song options. She ran through the litany of usual subjects. Heartache, cheating, love, money, drinking. There really were no original ideas, only remakes with a unique spin.

As she stepped out of the shower and reached for a towel, an idea struck—the new title of her next song ... *Absolutely*. A smile tugged at her lips as she pictured Corbin's face when he heard it. The lyrics floated through her mind, fitting together like pieces of a puzzle. She pursed her lips, staring at her reflection. How would she frame the song? It could go something like ...

Will you be there to hug me in the night? Absolutely.

Will you still love me in the morning light? Absolutely.

I'll absolutely love you ... for the rest of my life ... until the stars fall from the sky.

They say I'm damaged goods, and I admit it absolutely, but baby you give me more hope than a person ever should.

She tried to think of the rest, but that's all that would come. Now she wanted to hurry up and get ready so she could jot those notes down before they flew out of her mind. It was rough, but at least it was a start.

She blow-dried her hair and brushed it a few times, wishing she didn't have to put on the wig. She applied her makeup and rolled on lipgloss rather than lipstick. Then she put on the wig and fluffed the top like Marissa had instructed. The last thing she did before heading downstairs was put on a pair of dangly silver earrings. She studied her reflection, turning from side-to-side. It was amazing how much different she looked. She hardly recognized herself.

The tantalizing scent of bacon caused her stomach to rumble as she walked down the stairs. Her heart pounded out an erratic beat as she rubbed her sweaty palms on her jeans. She didn't have a clue what she'd say to Corbin. She stepped into the kitchen and the man turned, causing her to stop in her tracks.

"Wallace. I wasn't expecting you."

A friendly smile split his face, causing the wrinkles around his eyes to deepen. "Good morning. I hope you don't mind, but I thought I'd make breakfast."

She looked at the stack of pancakes beside the stove. Wallace slid the spatula under the pancake cooking in the skillet, turning it over with a flick of his wrist. "Where's Corbin?" She'd not expected him to leave without telling her where he'd gone. Was he ticked at her because of last night? Her heart dropped. *Probably.*

"He went to the store … something about buying some sausage and flour for biscuits and getting a certain little lady a decent set of pajamas."

"Oh." Wow. Impressive. Here she was thinking Corbin had left her high and dry and he was doing something nice. Guilt washed over her. She hated how she was always so quick to assume the worst about men. She thought of something. "How did Corbin get out in all the snow? The roads must be iced over." In Alabama, everything shut down when there were a few inches of snow; she couldn't imagine what it would be like with several feet.

"The private drive leading out to the main road's a little dicey because it doesn't get plowed. But everything else is clear."

"Does anything ever shut down because of the snow?"

"Not normally, unless we have a blizzard."

As far as Delaney was concerned, it had come a blizzard. But Wallace was acting like the storm was a normal event. Then again, it was Colorado.

"The ski resort will be happy to get the snow. We've had a dry winter." He motioned. "Have a seat."

"Can I help with anything?"

"Thanks, but it's ready." He slid the pancake to the top of the stack, then turned off the stovetop, wiping his hands on a dishtowel.

Delaney scooted out a chair, wincing when it made a loud scraping noise against the wood floor. "Sorry."

"Don't mind that. I've been meaning to put some new pads underneath the chair legs, but I haven't gotten around to it." Wallace placed the platter of pancakes in the center of the table. Before Delaney sat down, he held up a finger. "Oh, I forgot the orange juice. Would you mind getting it out of the fridge?"

"Not at all." She went to the fridge and retrieved it, suddenly realizing how hungry she was. She and Corbin had grabbed a quick sandwich for dinner the night before, eating it in the SUV as Corbin drove. Not super hungry, Delaney had only eaten half of it. But now that she was in a safe, comfortable place, her appetite had returned with a vengeance. She placed the juice on the table, then sat down.

Wallace put the syrup, butter, and bacon on the table before joining her. "Sorry we don't have any whipped cream. I forgot to get that when I went shopping."

She reached for a napkin, placing it in her lap. "This looks great." She was about to reach for a pancake, then stopped when Wallace bowed his head to pray.

Quickly, she closed her eyes and lowered her head, embarrassed that she'd forgotten. She needed the Lord's help to see her through this situation and didn't want to be one of those people who only prayed when desperate. Wallace named everything he was grateful for, even expressing thanks that she was here. "Please keep Dee and Corbin safe," he implored.

Tears wet her eyes, an unexpected warmth filling her chest. Maybe everything would turn out okay, after all.

"And please bless Dee and Corbin to understand their feelings and come together as a righteous couple in thy sight." He ended the prayer with a hearty "Amen."

"Amen," Delaney mumbled, opening her eyes. She wasn't sure what to make of that last part. Wallace knew her situation, was aware that the boyfriend/girlfriend thing was a façade. Why in the heck was he praying for them to come together as a couple? She gave him a questioning look, but he seemed totally oblivious.

He shook out his napkin before placing it in his lap. "Dig in."

She filled her plate with two pancakes and two slices of bacon. Then she placed a pat of butter on top and spread it with her fork before pouring on a generous amount of syrup. She cut off a section of the pancakes and placed them in her mouth, appreciating how they melted. She couldn't remember the last time she'd tasted pancakes this good ... if ever. "These are delicious."

"Thanks," Walter beamed. "I love big breakfasts, but Addie leaves so early for work that there's no time to eat. I don't like going to the trouble of cooking up a lot of food for just me, so I usually have coffee and toast. This is a welcome change."

"Well, I'm glad I can be the beneficiary of your skill." She bit off a section of crunchy bacon, chewing appreciatively.

"I'm sure you were wondering about my prayer."

The bacon went down the wrong pipe. Delaney coughed to clear it. She'd only thought he was oblivious. *The sly dog.* Wallace was direct like Corbin. Or maybe it was vice versa. "Yeah, it took me off guard," she admitted. "Especially since you know my situation."

He took a long swig of juice and placed the glass down with an audible plunk. Then he took a large bite of pancakes. He seemed to be deliberately chewing, making her wait for his response.

"I watched the two of you together last night, could tell there's a lot more brewing than a pretend relationship." He took another drink of juice.

A shaky laugh escaped her throat as she touched her neck which felt hot enough to combust. "Maybe we're just good at acting."

"I don't think so." He pinned her with a look. "You care about my grandson, maybe even love him."

She belted out a laugh, then clamped her lips shut to cut it off. "Love him? I hardly know him. We've only been together for a few days."

He shrugged. "Time is irrelevant when it comes to matters of the heart. Did Corbin ever tell you how Lou Ella and I met?"

"No."

"We were at the county fair. Lou Ella was with a date, standing by the Ferris Wheel. I saw her and my world shifted. She was the most beautiful woman I'd ever laid eyes on. She looked at me and we had this connection ... something that defied words." His eyes sparkled. "I knew in that moment that I'd move heaven and earth to be with her."

She jerked slightly, the irony not lost on her as she thought of the strong connection she and Corbin had when they first saw each other. "How could you be so sure that the two of you were meant to be together?"

He shrugged. "I don't know. But I knew it to the depth of my soul. Lou Ella knew it too." He grinned. "But it took a while before I could get her to admit it. I must've asked her out a hundred times, but she turned me down. That's okay though, because I'm persistent. I knew I'd eventually win her over."

Was that how Corbin felt about her? Would he be as persistent? A spark of warmth shot through her as she realized that she hoped he would. A tumult of feelings rushed through her, feelings she didn't fully understand. Since moving to San Diego she'd found a church to attend, one where she felt welcome. Pastor Simmons was always saying that the Lord's time is not the same as ours. And that He works in mysterious ways. Maybe the Lord had put Corbin in her path for more than just protection from her awful situation. Her eyes misted as she blinked a few times to clear the emotion. "That's a beautiful story. Thanks for telling it to me."

"Absolutely."

She smiled at the reference.

Wallace's voice grew reflective. "This coming May, Lou Ella and I'll celebrate our fiftieth wedding anniversary."

"Congratulations."

A trace of sadness flitted over his features. "I only wish Lou Ella realized."

"I'm sorry. Corbin told me about her Alzheimer's." The depth of feeling in Wallace's eyes struck something inside Delaney. This wasn't some storybook romance that would vanish like the dew at sunrise. She got the distinct feeling that what Wallace and Lou Ella had was deep and abiding ... a love that would transcend age, even death. When she was younger before Tuck's cruelty had jaded her, Delaney had wished for something like this. She'd held onto that dream to stave off the loneliness that consumed her, while her mother was passed out cold in the next room. Sure, the timing was lousy, but what if Corbin was the very thing she'd been searching for her entire life? A haven for her heart.

He nodded. "Before Lou Ella got sick, she had a memory like an elephant. She was smart and loved to read, would devour every book she could get her hands on. She was always helping, tending to someone who was sick, making casseroles. She loved to bake and crochet. In fact, she made the green afghan over the back of the couch."

Delaney had been so exhausted the night before that she'd not paid much attention to the furnishings. She made a mental note to look at the afghan. "Lou Ella sounds like a remarkable woman."

"Her greatest strength was her kindness. She and Corbin were really close." He paused, his jaw working. "It nearly killed Corbin when Lou Ella went into the care center." His eyes moistened. "It hurt me too, but I didn't see any other option. Lou Ella's condition was deteriorating to the point where she was becoming belligerent. She'd get out of the house while I was asleep. One night, I found her wandering in the snow. I was worried about her safety."

There was a hint of pleading in Wallace's voice, like he was defending himself. He felt guilty for putting Lou Ella in the care center. Delaney was surprised Wallace was telling her such personal things. Maybe he didn't get much of a chance to talk to other people. The cabins were in a remote area and Addie worked a lot. "I'm sure you did what you thought was best."

"Yes." He hesitated like he wanted to say more but didn't know if he should.

She leaned forward slightly. "What else?" The instant the question left her mouth, she thought she probably shouldn't have asked it, but she did want to know the rest. And Wallace certainly seemed like he needed to get it off his chest.

"I wish Corbin could understand."

"I'm sure he does, how could he not?"

"My grandson's very stubborn."

"Tell me about it," she chuckled.

"The two of us don't always get along." A rueful smile touched his lips. "Lou Ella used to say it was because we were too much alike."

"I can see that, even just now getting to know you."

"You're good for Corbin. For some time, he's been drifting. I'd hoped joining the military would help anchor him, but it only seems to have exacerbated the problem."

"Because of what happened to Doug?"

A look of surprise washed over him. "You know about Doug?"

"Yes, Corbin told me about him and the little girl."

He cocked his head. "What girl?"

Crap! She assumed that Wallace knew. *Time to backpedal. Fast.* She could feel Wallace's perceptive eyes, scrutinizing her. She put down her fork, shaking her head. "I'm sorry, I thought you knew. But if Corbin didn't tell you, I don't think it's my place to say anything." Her voice dribbled off.

Wallace nodded in disappointment. "I understand. And I certainly wouldn't want you to divulge a confidence."

She sought for the words to smooth over the situation. "I'm sure he'll tell you if you ask."

He gave her a sad smile that said, *You don't have a clue what you're talking about.* "Corbin would've told Lou Ella and she could've helped him sort through his feelings. Now that she's not in her right mind ..." he sighed "... well, it's just been festering." He paused, looking thoughtful. Then a new light came into his eyes. "But he told you."

"Yes," she said quietly, just now understanding the significance of all that had taken place the night before. She could argue that Corbin had told her due to circumstance. She came in right after the dream. No, Wallace was right. Corbin had opened his heart to her and she'd pushed him away.

"Like I said, you're good for Corbin. You give him a sense of purpose, make him want to be a better man. I'm so grateful he has you in his life."

Panic fluttered in her stomach. "No, I can't take on that responsibility." She'd tried to help her mother, but everything had blown up in her face. The harder she tried to get her mother off alcohol and drugs, the more her mother hated her for it. Her voice grew brittle. "I can't help Corbin because I can't even help myself." Tears burned her eyes. "I'm sorry." She pushed back her plate, no longer hungry. "I'm a train wreck," she muttered. She scooted her chair back to leave, but Wallace caught her arm.

"Hey." His voice was gentle but authoritative like he was talking a jumper off a ledge. His eyes held hers. "Don't run off. Just hear me out, okay?"

Tears dribbled down her cheeks. "Okay." He let go of her arm as she sat back down, wiping at the tears.

"While I don't know all the details of your situation, I know your ex-husband was abusive."

She gave him a curt nod of acknowledgement as shame burned through her. She crossed her arms tightly over her chest, her eyes fixed on her uneaten plate of food. If only she'd had enough sense not to get involved with Tuck. Yes, she'd finally summoned the courage to stand up to him and look where it had gotten her—on the run for her life from a demon even worse than Tuck.

Wallace leaned back in his seat. "Do you know much about the Native Americans indigenous to Colorado? They're known as the Plains Indians, making up several tribes. Shoshone, Apache, Navajo to name a few."

"No." She couldn't imagine where this was headed.

"I have a close friend Sani who's Navajo. I allow him to hunt on my property. He's really good with the bow. Killed an eight-point-buck. The thing was monstrous." He held out his hands. "The rack was this wide." He stopped, giving her a sheepish grin. "You don't care about hunting, do you?"

"Not really," she admitted, "but I know plenty about it. I grew up in Alabama, after all."

He was impressed. "Do you know how to shoot?"

A smile flickered over her lips. "Like I said, I'm from Alabama."

"Corbin's a sharpshooter. Another thing the two of you have in common."

"I'm not a sharpshooter by any stretch of the imagination, but I know how to handle a gun."

He grinned. "I knew I liked you. Oh, Corbin can sing too."

"Really?" Now that she found intriguing.

"He has a great voice, can even play the guitar."

"I had no idea."

"See, the two of you are more alike than you realize." He smiled broadly. "You're a great singer, by the way. I watched you on YouTube."

The admiration in his voice was touching. No matter how many times people gave her compliments on her music, it never got old. In some small way, every time she took the stage she healed a small part of herself because performing was the one thing she could be proud of—evidence that she'd broken out of the bonds of her childhood and made something of herself, despite all obstacles. "Thanks."

"The wig doesn't look bad on you, but I like your real hair much better."

"Me too." She touched her wig, wondering why she was wearing it in the cabin when the only other person here right now knew who she was. Then again, someone could see her through the windows or drop by the cabin unannounced. *Better to be safe than sorry.*

He waved a hand. "Anyway, back to the story, Sani once told me something that stuck with me. A grandfather was speaking to his grandson telling him how every living person has two wolves within … warring for dominance. The first is anger, fear, greed, malice. The other is kindness, benevolence, hope, faith. 'But Grandfather, which wolf will win?' the grandson asked."

Delaney waited for the rest, but Wallace just sat there, studying her. She was starting to recognize a pattern here. Wallace wanted her to be an active learner—giving the answer only when she was ready to receive it. A smile touched her lips as she asked the question dutifully. "What did the grandfather say?" *Two wolves inside every person. An interesting concept.* It certainly described her. Even as the thoughts rolled through her mind, she could feel something building inside her, knew somehow that Wallace's answer would be significant.

"Which wolf will survive?" His tone was light, musing, a direct contrast to the intensity in his eyes. "The one you feed."

16

Birchwood Springs really does need better places for shopping, Corbin thought as he pulled into the driveway of the cabin. He went to three different shops and couldn't find any decent pajamas. Finally, he settled on a pair of sweats and a t-shirt. Delaney would probably think he was crazy for going shopping, but he was just trying to think of something nice to do for her ... something to let her know that he wasn't a bad guy.

After she left his room the night before, he'd lain awake thinking about their conversation and the kiss. He thought he might regret telling Delaney about what happened in the Philippines, but he didn't. He wanted her to know everything about him, as he wanted to know about her.

He reached for the bags and transferred them all to his left hand, then grabbed the bouquet of flowers with his right. On impulse, he'd grabbed the flowers as he was leaving the grocery store. Was it too much? He hoped not.

As he walked to the door, his skin prickled with the knowledge that someone was watching him. He looked at the cabin to his right, about half a football field away. A man had gotten out of his car, also going into his cabin. When he realized that Corbin had made eye contact, he smiled and waved. Corbin nodded and offered a brief smile. The heavyset man was bald and looked to be in his early sixties. He seemed harmless, but under the circumstance Corbin had to be cautious about everyone.

"Hey," Pops said when he stepped into the cabin. Pops was reclining on the couch, watching TV with his hands behind his head, his feet propped on the coffee table.

"Hey." Corbin looked around. "Where's Delaney?" He hoped she hadn't been too upset when she realized he was gone. She was sleeping so peacefully when he left that he hated to wake her. And, he needed some time to sort through things, try to figure out the best way to get through to Delaney. What he most wanted at this point was for her to give him a chance.

"In her room, working on songs."

Corbin placed the bags on the kitchen table and began removing the groceries, then placed the perishables in the refrigerator. "Who's the guy next door? The portly bald guy?"

"Oh, that's Gus Ridley."

"Do you know him very well?"

"Yes, he and his wife Jean have been coming here for years."

Good to hear. He didn't have to worry about the man.

"Why do you ask?"

"He was outside as I came in. He waved. I just wondered."

"It's good to be vigilant, considering the situation."

"Exactly."

"Nice flowers," Pops said a few seconds later.

Corbin looked at the colorful bouquet in question, caught the teasing in Pops' voice, but he chose to ignore it. "Thanks," he said lightly. He went to the cupboards. "Is there a vase, or something I can put these in?"

"There's a Mason Jar on the top shelf, to the right of the microwave. I saw it when I was making breakfast."

"Oh, yeah. How was breakfast?"

"Great. There are leftovers in the fridge if you want them."

"That's okay. I ran by a drive-through and grabbed something before I went shopping." He reached for the jar and filled it with water. The flowers were wrapped in plastic. A packet of flower food was attached to the stems with a rubber band. He pulled out several drawers. "What about scissors?"

"There should be some in there. I asked Hilda to stock all the cabins with them."

"Found 'em." He cut off the rubber band and removed the plastic. Corbin didn't know the first thing about arranging flowers. He grabbed the stems and stuffed them into the jar all at once. He stepped back to admire his handiwork. He frowned. It looked pathetic, like a blob. Maybe he should've left the flowers in the plastic. He shifted them around a little, but it didn't seem to help. Oh, well. It was the thought that counted, right? He was a bodyguard, not a florist. Oops, he forgot to add the food. He snipped a corner of the packet, and pushed the stems to the side, then emptied the powder into the water.

He placed the flowers in the center of the table where Delaney couldn't miss them. Then he sat down beside Pops. "Thanks for holding down the fort."

"Sure. I enjoyed spending time with Dee. She's a good girl. We had a great conversation."

He kept his tone casual. "What did you guys talk about?"

"Oh, you know. Life. Relationships ... stuff like that."

He tensed. "What sort of relationships?"

Pops reached for the remote and turned down the volume on the TV. Then he angled toward Corbin. He arched an eyebrow, a trace of defiance in his expression. "You really wanna know?"

"Well, yeah. I wouldn't have asked if I didn't." It was crazy how fast the irritation surfaced.

"We talked about you and her."

The breath left Corbin's lungs. His eyes narrowed. "What're you up to, Pops? You have no right to meddle in my personal life."

"On the contrary. I have every right. You called and asked for my help, remember? Came here."

It was just like Pops to throw that in his face. "Yeah, I wanted to bring Delaney, Dee," he corrected, "here to keep her safe, not for you to play matchmaker." There was no telling what Pops told her.

"Aren't you interested in what she said?"

"Well ... yeah." Pops had him and he knew it. He desperately wanted to know what Delaney said, but he wasn't about to give Pops the satisfaction of begging.

A sly smile slid over Pops' lips. "She likes you. A lot."

"Really?" Hope rose in his chest. "She said that."

"Yeah. Not in those exact words, but that was the inference."

He gave Pops a hard look. "Are you sure you didn't misconstrue the conversation?"

"Absolutely. Dee cares about you, but she's scared because of what happened with her ex."

"She told you that?" He was surprised that Pops had gotten Delaney to open up to him. And he was a little envious too.

Pops winked. "Given enough time, I think she'll come around."

"I wouldn't be so sure," Corbin said darkly. "She's been hurt bad. I don't know if she'll ever be able to trust anyone else."

"Just be patient with her. You'll see ... it'll work out."

He could tell Pops really believed that. Corbin wished he could be as sure.

Pops sat up straight and cleared his throat. "There's something else I want to talk to you about."

"Okay." Wariness settled over him. This sounded serious. "What is it?"

"This guy that's after Dee, he's bad news, huh?"

"Yeah, Hugh Allen's the worst of the worst."

"How are you gonna stop him?"

He tightened his fist. "I'm going to do everything in my power to keep Delaney safe, if that's what you're asking." Was Pops questioning his ability? Of course he was. He never believed that Corbin could do anything right.

Pops looked him in the eye. "So you're gonna spend the rest of your life running?"

He rocked back. "I'm not sure what you're getting at."

"If this guy's as ruthless as you say, he won't stop until he finds you and Dee."

Corbin rolled his eyes. "I'm glad to see you have so little faith in me," he said sarcastically.

Pops cocked his head. "Is that what you think?"

"Yeah, quite frankly, that's exactly what I think." They stared at one other, all the old hurts and disagreements boiling to the top. Corbin was surprised to see a twitch in Pops' jaw, then moisture in his eyes.

"Nothing could be further from the truth." He placed a hand on Corbin's arm. "I know we haven't always seen eye-to-eye, but I want you to know how proud of you I am."

The words broadsided Corbin like a fist to the gut. He couldn't ever remember Pops giving him an outright compliment. Emotion rumbled in his throat as he swallowed.

"I know you've been through some hard times," Pops continued, "but I want you to know that the proudest moment of my life was when you were serving your country. I don't know what happened out there, but I know you. I know your heart. You're a good man." His voice hitched. "But you're also a hard, stubborn fool. Just like me. You may think that you'll never be able to get past what happened to you, but you will. That's the greatest gift the good Lord gave us ... the power to change ... to start again. I changed for that amazing, good-hearted woman in the care center, and I know you can do the same for Dee."

Tears brimmed in Corbin's eyes, blurring his vision.

"I should've told you that a long time ago."

Corbin coughed to cover the emotion.

Pops smiled thinly. "I guess with your grandmother around, I didn't have to. She could take up the slack. But now that she's ... sick ... well, things are different."

"I miss her," Corbin said quietly, the ache in his gut so powerful he could hardly contain it.

"I miss her too, son." A tear dribbled down Pops' cheek. "She loved you. In her eyes, the sun rose and set with you."

Corbin looked down at the floor. He loved her too, so much that it cut to the quick.

"Back to this thing with Hugh Allen." Pops cleared his throat, his jaw tightening.

Corbin recognized that gesture well. Pops was bottling up his emotion and putting on the hard cap. That he'd said as much as he had was a miracle.

"You can't keep running. You and Dee have to face him."

He barked out a laugh, hardly believing what he was hearing. "Why? So he can kill Delaney?"

"So you can put an end to this thing. Better to do it on your own turf rather than on someone else's." He lifted his chin, his eyes going hard. "You'll stand more of a chance facing him here than anywhere else."

Corbin shook his head. As frustrated as he got with his grandfather, he admired his torque. Pops believed he was invincible. Sure he was tough, part of that generation that breathed grit and determination. He'd taught Corbin how to fish, how to hunt, how to shoot, how to suck it up and be a man. But Pops had no idea what he was up against here. An image of the little girl flashed through his mind. It was still fresh from the nightmare. The white dress, the mother's anguished cry, the blood spilling out. A shudder went through him. He could never intentionally put Delaney in harm's way. "No, I can't do that."

"It's the only way to keep her safe. Remember the story of the bear?"

A laugh scratched Corbin's throat. Pops and his never-ending parables. "I don't wanna hear the stupid bear story, all right?"

Pops rubbed a hand across his brow. "Fine, but you're not thinking about this sensibly."

His grandfather was a stubborn old fool. Corbin's voice rose. "You'd really have me lure Hugh and his goons here? What about you? And Addie?"

Pops' face paled.

Checkmate. Pops hadn't thought about that, what it would mean for their family. Maybe he'd realize now and drop the whole thing.

"You said your boss has endless resources. We could tap into those to help fight this."

He shook his head. The man was unbelievable, like a dog refusing to let go of a bone. "Pops, this isn't some game. This is serious—a life and death situation. Sutton, my boss, is taking precautions. When I first found out about Delaney's situation, I wanted to rush in and take care of Hugh, but Sutton said it would be too dangerous—too much collateral damage. That we should wait and let Hugh come to us." After thinking about it, Corbin wondered if Sutton's hesitancy to charge after Hugh was also owed to principle. It was one thing to act out of protection and another altogether to be the aggressor. Heaven favored the former, and Sutton seemed to be a God-fearing man.

Pops clenched his fist. "Exactly," he exclaimed, like Corbin had just gotten it. "You lure the bear out of the protection of its cave."

"But that doesn't mean we should bring the danger to our doorstep. Do you have some sort of death wish?"

"No, I do not," he countered stiffly. "And I don't appreciate your tone. I'm only trying to protect you and Dee."

He blew out a breath. "So am I, Pops. So am I," he repeated quietly. He looked at his aged grandfather, feeling a wave of sympathy for him. "Look, I appreciate your help, but you need to let me do this my way. Sutton has everything under control on his end, and so do I." He gave Pops a firm look. "Okay? I'm a big boy. I don't need you or anyone else running my life."

Pops nodded, but Corbin could tell he wasn't convinced. Corbin stood to leave, but Pops caught his arm. He cleared his throat, hesitation washing over him. "There's something I need to talk to you about."

He sat back down.

"You need to go and visit your grandmother." His features clouded. "She's not doing well."

Corbin rocked back, eyes narrowing. "Well, of course she's not well. You've got her stuffed away in that place." The words dripped like daggers from his lips as he shot Pops an accusing look. While a part of him understood why Gram had to be there, the larger part of him couldn't. No that wasn't true. This didn't have as much to do with Pops as it did with himself. Guilt was eating him alive. Corbin was the worst offender of all. He'd left when Gram got sick because he couldn't stand watching her wither away.

Pops' features tightened making him look older, a shriveled banana skin. Then Corbin saw the compassion in his eyes, realized it was directed at him. Without warning, tears rose in Corbin's eyes.

"I know Lou Ella's sickness has been hard on you."

Heavy emotion pressed like cement on Corbin's chest. He couldn't handle this right now. He had to keep his mind focused on keeping Delaney safe. His personal issues would have to wait.

"I think if you'll just go and see Lou Ella, it'll help you come to terms with what's happening to her."

Corbin sprang to his feet, unwilling to let the avalanche of emotion smother him. "I'm going to check on Delaney," he said gruffly, turning his back to Pops. He sucked in a breath, brushing at his tears with jerky swipes. "Thanks for taking care of things while I stepped out." His voice cracked as he fought for control. "Don't feel like you have to stick around. I know you've got plenty of things to take care of."

He rushed out of the room before Pops could see him lose it.

17

The song was coming, but not as quickly as Delaney wanted. That was mostly because her thoughts kept returning to Corbin and the conversation she'd had earlier with Wallace. The wolf analogy really hit home. No doubt she'd been feeding the wrong wolf because it had been howling the loudest. Could she stop feeding it? Silence her fears once and for all? Oh, how she wanted to.

It was interesting how closely her and Corbin's first meeting paralleled Wallace and Lou Ella's. They'd had an instant attraction and it morphed into something wonderful and lasting. Could that happen to her and Corbin? At this point, the best she could hope for was to open up a small space in her heart for the beginnings of a relationship. Take things one step at a time. Her next thought sent her into a tailspin. Was Corbin even interested in a lasting relationship or was she merely a form of amusement, a way to pass the time? Never again would she take anything at face value. She had to find out what Corbin's true intentions were before she could even entertain the idea of a relationship.

She pushed aside the intrusive thoughts, turning her attention back to the song as she strummed her guitar.

They say I'm damaged goods, and I admit it absolutely, but baby
  you give me more hope than a person ever should.

I've got to learn to silence these fears and dry my tears.

Will you be there to hug me in the night?

Will you still love me in the morning light?

I'll absolutely love you ... for the rest of my life ... until the stars fall
  from the sky.

She heard movement, realized Corbin was leaning against the
doorframe. Her heart turned a cartwheel. He looked amazing in
jeans and a snug sweater that stretched across his pecs. His messy
hair was begging for her to run her fingers through it. She took in his
lean jaw and arresting eyes, which were sparkling with amusement,
making them look more amber. Wait a minute! The more she studied
him, the more she got the feeling there was something off about
Corbin. The rims of his eyes were a bit red like he might've been
crying. Then again, he didn't act like he'd been crying. He was probably just tired. They'd been under a mountain of stress. It was bound
to take its toll eventually.

"Are you doing okay?"

He looked surprised. "Yeah, why?"

She tipped her head. "I dunno. You just look a little sad."

He pursed his lips, shoving his hands in his pockets. "I'm good."
With that, the last traces of despondency vanished, making her
wonder if she'd only imagined it. "I like the song." His grin gave way
to a full smile as he repeated the lyrics. "I'll absolutely love you ...
until the stars fall from the sky."

Heat tinged her cheeks. She hated that she always blushed when
she was embarrassed. Once the song was recorded, it would be on
display for the world. Why was she feeling sheepish about Corbin
hearing it now? The answer came to her in an instant. Because he

knew she was talking about him, that's why. In her music she was most transparent, her innermost feelings coming to the surface.

She caught the pleased look on his face. Were his feelings for her real? "You forgot a segment."

He sat down at the foot of the bed. "Oh?"

"I'll absolutely love you ... for the rest of my life ... until the stars fall from the sky."

The hope in his eyes sparked something inside her. This had to be real! No one was that good at pretending. Even when she was with Tuck, a part of her knew he was only pretending to be appalled by his brother's behavior. Tuck had a reputation for being rough. She'd turned a blind eye to the rumors because she wanted so desperately for him to be her knight in shining armor. And, back then, Tuck and Hugh's behavior was more a part of everyday life. It wasn't until she got away from it that she realized how truly warped they were and how mixed up her own mother had been.

"I like it." Corbin gave her a searching look. "I'd like to hear the rest."

"Do you think Wallace will mind me using *Absolutely*? It has such a catchy ring to it."

"I'm sure Pops will be honored." He looked down at her notebook of lyrics and chords. "Is the song finished yet?"

"It's getting close. I haven't written the last verse and there are still a few tweaks to work out, but I'm pleased with the progress."

"Sounds like you and Pops had a nice breakfast."

She sensed his interest, even though he was trying hard to act nonchalant.

"Yes, we did." She chuckled lightly. "He has some great stories."

"That he does." Corbin leaned forward and reached for her pencil, absently twirling it in his fingers. "What did the two of you talk about?"

It was Delaney's turn to be amused. "He didn't tell you?"

His lips drew together. "Nope."

"Well, one of the things he mentioned is that you play the guitar and sing."

His eyes widened. "He told you that?"

She couldn't stop a smile from stretching over her lips. "Yep. Said you're not half bad."

He grunted. "Half bad, huh?"

She laughed. "Nah, just teasing. He said you were good." Her eyes held his. "But I'd have to hear it to believe it."

"Is that right?"

"Yep." Maybe she was playing with fire, but she wanted to get to know Corbin and was tired of putting up so many barriers. She didn't want to spend her life alone. She was tired of feeding the wrong wolf. There was that darn analogy again, but it had hit home. "Care to join me?" Her heart picked up a beat as she waited for his reaction.

A brilliant smile broke across his lips, causing her to lose her train of thought for a second. "I thought you'd never ask." He got up and sat beside her.

Her heart hammered against her ribcage and she wondered if he could hear it. *Sheesh!* With him this close, it was hard to concentrate. His scent was clean and masculine with a hint of mint.

He reached for the paper. "Okay, what you got?"

She sat up straight, her back resting against the headboard as she started from the beginning. After the first round of the chorus, he joined in. His baritone voice was full and rich. They harmonized automatically, him taking over the melody while she played around with the harmonies. Like Wallace said, Corbin was good. The entire time they sang, all she could think about was that these lyrics offered a clear window into her heart, letting him know that she was having some strong feelings for him. Maybe it was good that they were singing. She could express herself better through music than dialogue. When the song ended, she put down the guitar and turned to face him. "What do you think?"

His eyes were riveted to hers and in them she saw desire swirled with a tenderness that sang to her heart. In this moment, her fears were soothed in a manner she'd not thought possible. "I love it," Corbin uttered. Her breath caught when he touched her cheek. His finger trailed along her lips, lightly tracing their outline. A tender ache grew in her throat as she leaned closer. This time, it was her lips that touched his first, moving softly and cautiously until he deepened the kiss, pulling her into his arms.

The need for him was intoxicating, sending scrumptious quivers tingling down her spine as she buried her hands in his messy hair that her fingers had been longing to touch. His lips were hard, demanding, but she met him measure for measure, reveling in the way her spirit soared to the sky. Kissing Corbin was more thrilling than a thousand concerts all rolled into one.

Finally, he pulled back. His magnetic eyes burning with intensity as he searched her face. "Please tell me that wasn't pretend."

She laughed lightly, resting her palms on his chest, taking note of his rock-hard muscles. "No."

He touched her wig. "Can I take this off? So I can feel your real hair?"

Delicious shivers danced through her. "Absolutely."

They both laughed as he attempted to remove the wig, but the combs were embedded deep in her hair. She let out a tiny yelp at the pain of her hair being pulled.

"Sorry. I better let you do it."

She took off the wig and hair net, then ran her fingers through her hair, which she was sure was an absolute mess.

"Let me do that." His hands went up the back of her neck, into her hair. "Much better," he murmured, his lips taking hers once more.

When the kiss was over, he rested his forehead against hers. His hands went to her arms as he rubbed them up and down. "You're incredible."

"You're not so bad yourself."

He pulled back, searching her face. She could tell he wanted to say something. "What?" she asked.

Concern trickled into his eyes. She swallowed, her fears returning with a vengeance. "What is it?"

"I want to tell you something, but I don't want you to freak out."

"Okay." *Geez.* He'd not even told her the bad news yet, and she was already freaking out.

"I'm falling hard for you."

It took a second for her mind to process what he'd said. A warm glow settled over her.

He tightened his hold. "Don't retreat. Please."

She was giddier than a bubbly teenager, unable to hold back the laugh in her throat. "That was your bad news?"

He looked puzzled. "I never said the news was bad. Just that I wanted to tell you something and didn't want you to freak out."

She cupped his face. "Why? Because I've been feeding the wrong wolf for so long?"

His eyes rounded as he laughed. "You have been talking to Pops."

"A little. You know, he's a smart guy, you should pay more attention to his advice."

"Ha. I'll have to remember that."

Was it her imagination or did a cloud move over his features? It was gone in the next instant as he searched her face. "So, does this mean you're good with what's happening between us?"

"That depends."

He tensed. "On what?"

"On what this is." She eyed him. "Is this a real thing, or am I a distraction ... something to keep you occupied while we're stuck in this cabin?"

An incredulous laugh left his throat. "Is that what you think?"

She thought for a minute. "No. I think your feelings for me are real. I just wanna hear it from you. I made a grave mistake before, and I'm not about to make that same mistake again."

He frowned. "I'm not Tuck."

"I know."

His voice gathered intensity. "What I feel for you is real, more real than anything I've felt before."

The truth of his words settled around her like a protective cocoon as she snuggled into the curve of his shoulder. He linked his fingers through hers, squeezing her hand. "I'm starting to care about you too," she admitted. There was one other question she wanted to ask. "So, have there been other girls that you've guarded? Ones you've spent lots of time with?" She held her breath, waiting for an answer, realizing that she was starting to care a great deal about him ... maybe even love him a little.

"No."

Relief splattered over her as she turned to face him. "Really?"

A trace of amusement lit his eyes. "Really. You're the first person I've ever protected."

She frowned. "But I thought you had a long history of working in security."

"I do, but mostly for bars and institutions, not for individuals. Sutton offered me the job the night of the party." He paused. "Does that make you nervous? That I'm new at this one-on-one stuff?"

A feeling of bliss danced over her. "On the contrary, I think it's great that I'm your first assignment."

He turned to face her, the fervency in his eyes making her wonder if he could see into her soul. "The word assignment doesn't even begin to describe what you are to me." His lips turned up in a slight smile.

"What?"

"At the risk of sending you running for the hills, let me just say that from the first moment our eyes connected across that crowded room, I knew we'd end up together." He studied her. "Does it scare you that I'm so certain?"

"A little," she admitted, but his words were thrilling at the same time. "Maybe it runs in the family, like Wallace and Lou Ella at the fair."

He laughed. "Wow, Pops rolled out an entire volume of the Spencer family history in one sitting. That must've been a long breakfast."

"Long enough to get the goods on you," she teased.

"Oh, no. Now I'm worried."

She rested her head against him, savoring how safe she felt in his arms.

"So," he began, "are you feeling a little cooped up in the cabin?"

"I was earlier, but I'm not now that you're here."

"You do say the most marvelous things," he said tightening his hold on her and kissing the top of her head. "What if I told you I have a surprise for you?"

Anticipation thrummed through her veins as she turned to look at him. "I love surprises. What is it?" she asked eagerly.

"Would you like to go skiing? At Bear Claw Resort?"

"Today?"

"Yeah, this afternoon. Addie can get us all fixed up with the gear."

The idea of learning how to ski was glorious. She wrinkled her nose. "But what if someone recognizes me?"

"That would be highly unlikely with your trusty wig, goggles, and a snow suit." His eyes sparked in a challenge. "You game?"

It only took her half a second to reach a decision. "Absolutely."

A crooked smile tugged at his lips making him look adorable. "You like that word, don't you?"

"Absolutely."

He groaned. "Pops started something." He removed his arm from her shoulders, sitting up. "All right. Put your wig back on, and let's get out of here." His voice quivered with excitement. "I can't wait to show you Birchwood Springs. There's no place more beautiful after a fresh snow. Afterwards, I thought you could make us some sausage gravy and biscuits."

"That sounds divine."

"Then," his voice went husky as he trailed a finger down the length of her hair, "I can make a fire and we can talk ..." his eyes lingered on her lips "... or practice."

A slow-burn tingled through her stomach. "Practice is great," she said softly, leaning in for another kiss.

18

For a rookie, Delaney was doing quite well. After a short tutorial by one of the instructors, she'd gone down the bunny slope. As soon as she did her first run, she pumped her fist victoriously in the air letting out a loud whoop. Corbin loved the fire in this girl.

"Are you ready for something a little more challenging?"

"Let me go down the bunny slope a couple more times, and I'll be ready. You wanna do this one with me?"

The excitement in her voice caused him to smile. Coming out here was a good idea, giving them both a chance to decompress. Delaney didn't know it, but before they left the cabin, Corbin had made a quick call to Sutton, verifying that Hugh and his men were still in Northern Cal. He explained that he was taking Delaney to Bear Claw Resort for the afternoon. He wanted Sutton to know where they'd be in case anything unexpected happened.

A couple hours later, they were in the lodge sitting in front of a toasty fire, their hands wrapped around steaming mugs of hot chocolate when Corbin glanced over and saw Madison Wells approaching. *Crap!* It had been against his better judgment to bring Delaney into the lodge, but she was cold and wanted something warm to drink. He wished he could jump up and take her out of here this instant. He cringed at the cheerful ring in Madison's voice. "Corbin Spencer, I didn't realize you were back in town." Madison was the blonde, peppy cheerleader type. Her voice oozed sweetness as she flashed a bright smile. Dutifully, Corbin stood as she stepped up to him and gave him a tight hug.

"Hey," she said in an intimate tone. "You should've called and let me know you were in town."

He stepped back, clearing his throat as he tightened his hold on the handle of the mug. He motioned at Delaney who rose to her feet. "Um, Madison, this is my girlfriend, Dee."

Madison's face tightened, going blistering red. She shot Delaney a vehement look then seemed to realize how she was coming across. A strained smile stretched over her face as she held out her hand. "Hello, it's nice to meet you."

Delaney slipped her free hand through Corbin's, stepping closer to him. "Nice to meet you too."

"You have the cutest accent," Madison said with such condescension that it made Corbin cringe. "Where are you from?"

"Alabama," Delaney shot back, giving her a steely look.

"Oh, Ala-bam-y," Madison twanged. "How cute."

Her phony Southern drawl grated on Corbin's nerves. Everything about Madison Wells got on his nerves, which was why he was so glad he'd ended things with her a long time ago.

Hurt clouded Madison's eyes. "I didn't realize you had a girlfriend." Before he could answer, she turned to Delaney looking her up and down. "Huh," she grunted.

"I beg your pardon," Delaney said. Corbin had to bite back a smile, loving how territorial Delaney was acting. He still couldn't believe that this stunning, amazing woman was with him.

Madison laughed. "Oh, I'm just surprised." Her lips turned down in a frown as she zeroed in on Delaney's hair. "Corbin has always preferred blondes." She flipped the ends of her shoulder-length platinum hair, giving Delaney a smug look.

Delaney turned to him, her eyes dancing. "Is that right? Good to know," she mused.

A bewildered expression crossed Madison's features. Corbin was ready for the diva to go away, but it was obvious that she had no intention of leaving just yet.

"I miss you, Cor," Madison drawled, thrusting out her lower lip into a petulant pout. She looked at Delaney, a conspiratorial chuckle rumbling in her throat as she touched Corbin's arm. "How strong is your relationship with Bea, anyway?"

"It's Dee," Corbin said firmly. "And it's ironclad."

Madison's face fell at the same time Delaney went rigid. Corbin was sure that if he looked at Delaney right now he'd see steam coming from her ears. Madison had always been catty, one of the reasons why the two of them didn't work out. That and she was too clingy. And bossy. About the only thing Madison Wells had going for her was her looks. But even then, she couldn't hold a candle to Delaney. And Delaney had class, whereas Madison didn't. Ironic considering Delaney was born into poverty and Madison with a silver spoon in her mouth. It just went to prove that true culture and class had more to do with the inner person than privileges they were given at birth.

"I'm just teasing," Madison purred, laughing lightly. Her brows furrowed as she studied Delaney. "Have we met before?"

"No," Delaney said stiffly.

Madison cocked her head. "You look so familiar. What's your last name?"

"Smith." Delaney tightened her hold on Corbin's arm. He glanced at her, noticing that her face had gone pale, alarm reflected in her eyes.

"I could swear I've seen you before … or someone like you," Madison continued. Corbin could feel the huntress going in for the kill.

"Maybe I look like someone you know," Delaney said.

"Maybe." Madison pursed her lips. "Hmm. It'll come to me. I never forget a face."

Silence dragged like a lead ball between them.

"Well," Madison finally said in a chipper, Bambi voice, "Nice meeting you, Dee." She smiled but her eyes remained cold. She looked at Corbin, her tone going silky. "Good to see you too, Cor." Before he realized what was happening, she leaned in and gave him a kiss on the lips. Then she patted his cheek and laughed. "One for old time's sake." She looked at Delaney. "Better hold onto him."

"Oh, I will," Delaney countered, a bite in her voice.

Madison sniffed and sauntered away.

When Delaney turned to him, her eyes were blazing. "So that was Madison Wells."

"Yep." He knew instinctively that the less he said, the better.

She put the mug of hot chocolate down on the side table. "Why did the two of you break up?"

The last thing he wanted to do was rehash his past relationships with Delaney. "Because Madison was controlling, vain, and not exactly the nicest person as you've just witnessed." He rolled his eyes.

She scoffed. "That's an understatement. I guess the more appropriate question is ... how in the heck did you ever pair up with her to begin with?"

He sighed. "She was a cheerleader, I was a football player. I was young."

A smile played on Delaney's lips. "And stupid."

"Yep, that too," he chuckled.

"Well, at least you had the good sense to get away from her."

"Amen to that." He turned to face her. "Had you been in the picture, I never would've started dating Madison."

Delaney blinked in surprise, a smile tipping her lips. "You're certainly charming."

"Just telling the truth." He glanced around, putting down the mug. "Now would be a good time for us to leave before someone recognizes you straight out."

"Good idea. That was a close call."

"Yeah, too close."

"Hey, you two. How did the skiing go?"

They turned as Addie stepped up to them.

They'd have a short conversation with Addie and then leave. "Really well," Corbin said. "Dela—Dee is a quick learner."

Delaney smiled. "Your brother's being very kind. I did okay on the bunny slope, but biffed it on the green circle. I'm sure I'll be sore tomorrow."

"You did great for your first run," Corbin said, and he meant it.

Addie tucked a loose curl behind her ear. "I had intented to look for you earlier, but it has been nonstop today, people coming in droves to take advantage of the fresh powder."

"No worries," Corbin assured her. He slid his arm around Delaney's waist. "We've been just fine."

"I can see that," Addie said, her eyes sparkling. She brought her hands together. "What are you doing tonight?"

"Oh, not too much," Corbin said evasively, not wanting to have to share Delaney with anyone. "Just spending time together. Couple stuff."

"Ah, I get it. Three's a crowd," Addie said.

"No, that's not the case at all," Delaney argued, red-faced.

"Yes, that's exactly the case," Corbin said firmly.

Delaney shoved him. "Hey, don't be rude to your sister."

"Thank you," Addie said, jutting out her chin. "I'm glad one of you appreciates me." She stuck her tongue out at Corbin.

"Hey, I appreciate you. I just wanna spend some time with my woman," he teased. Delaney was shooting him warnings with her eyes, but he just laughed.

"All right. I won't interrupt your little lovefest tonight, so long as you leave tomorrow afternoon open."

Corbin studied his little sister wondering what plan she was concocting in her curly head. "Why's that?"

"Because I'm taking off early and we're going to the care center to visit Gram."

Corbin sucked in an audible breath, dread pouring over him. "I don't think that'll work, sis." *Geez.* Pops and Addie were tag-teaming him. Why was it so important for him to visit the stupid care center? Gram wouldn't even know he was there.

Her hand flew to her hip, eyes narrowing. "Why not?"

"Delaney and I have other plans," he said crisply.

Addie shook her head. "Who's Delaney?"

He cleared his throat, his face going warm. *Oops.* He hadn't meant for that to slip out. Just as he feared, his personal hang-ups were clouding his judgment. "Um, I mean Dee."

"Oh." Addie looked back and forth between them, suspicion forming on her face. "Is there something going on that I need to know about?"

A streak of fear shot through Corbin. He glanced at Delaney who looked like she might pass out. He forced a smile. "No, sis. It's all good."

"Awesome. Then I'll meet you at the care center at three p.m. tomorrow." She jutted out her chin, daring him to disagree. "You can come too, Dee ... or Delaney."

"It's Dee," Corbin corrected sharply, "and I told you, tomorrow won't work."

"Maybe we should go to the care center."

He turned, surprised that Delaney had spoken.

She gave him a tender look. "We're all about fresh starts. It'll do you good to see your grandmother. And I'd like to meet her."

"You would?" he gulped.

"Absolutely."

It was amazing how fast Delaney had diffused the tension. Everything hung in the balance. He couldn't believe he was actually considering going. But he did want Delaney to meet Gram. "All right," he finally said. "We'll go." Had he really just agreed to this? Could he stand seeing Gram in her state? The truth was ... he wasn't sure, but knowing that Delaney would be by his side made the situation tolerable.

"Sounds good," Addie clipped. "See you both tomorrow." She patted Corbin's arm. "I've gotta run. You two enjoy the rest of your day ... and your lovefest," she cooed. When she got a couple of steps away from them, she turned and blew a kiss over her shoulder, laughter in her eyes.

"Lovefest, huh?" Delaney mused.

"I'm sorry about Addie," he began with a pained expression. "She can be a pill sometimes."

Delaney waved a hand. "No worries. I like her."

He tipped his head. "You do?"

"Yeah, she's got spunk." She chuckled. "She obviously knows how to put you in your place. Maybe I should get some pointers from her."

He laughed. "Oh, I think you do a pretty good job of putting me in my place all on your own." As he gazed into her mysterious dark eyes, he couldn't help but feel lucky. He would go to the end of the earth for Delaney Mitchell. Or to the care center, which was the harder task of the two.

19

As they drove to the care center, Delaney's mind skipped back to the previous night. Spending time with Corbin had been so glorious that her feet had hardly touched the ground since. It was crazy that she was feeling so joyous in the face of impending danger with Hugh. Biscuits were temperamental, especially at higher elevations, but they turned out perfect, as did the sausage and gravy. Corbin ate so much she was afraid he'd make himself sick.

Afterwards, they cuddled in front of a fire, sharing long, drugging kisses until late in the evening. Delaney was eager to find out everything she could about Corbin. She asked him questions about what it was like to grow up in Birchwood Springs. As he shared memories of growing up in a comfortable, stable home, she couldn't help but compare his upbringing with her chaotic past. She'd shared a few experiences with him ... how there was never much food in the trailer ... how the truancy officer was always on their case due to the large amount of school Delaney missed ... how there'd always been random men coming and going until Hugh entered the picture. She let out a bitter laugh. "To think, I was actually excited when Hugh Allen and my mom started seeing each other because we no longer had to worry about scraping rent money together. Hugh threw money around like it was paper, and I could buy whatever I wanted to eat." Corbin's expression had gone solemn as he pulled her into his arms and held her close. Just as she drifted off to sleep, she heard him say that he loved her.

She glanced at his rugged profile, his hands on the steering wheel. Corbin had been unusually quiet since they left the cabin. "Are you okay?"

For a second, he looked surprised that she'd spoken. Then an automatic smile crossed his lips. "Yeah."

But he wasn't okay. Fear clutched her. Was he having second thoughts about them? Maybe he regretted telling her that he loved her. She took in a breath, willing herself to calm down. She couldn't keep assuming the worst every second. Corbin was probably just nervous about visiting his grandmother.

He pulled into an empty parking space, taking in a deep breath. "Thanks for coming with me." A slight smile touched his lips. She reached for his hand, which was cold. "Do you wanna talk about it?" she asked, searching his face.

His lips pulled into a taut line. "No. I just wanna get this over with."

"When's the last time you came here?"

"Never."

Her eyes widened. Never? No wonder he was so keyed up. And no wonder Addie made such a big deal about him coming.

He got out of the SUV and came around to open her door. As he helped her out, she realized he was shaking. "It'll be all right," she said, putting a hand on his arm.

He nodded, forcing a smile. "Let's do this."

A middle-aged woman with a cap of shiny red hair and lipstick to match was sitting behind the reception desk. She smiled brightly in recognition as they walked through the door. "Corbin Spencer," she boomed. "This is a nice surprise. It's great to see you."

"Good to see you too, Tina," he said mechanically. She came around the desk and gave him a hug, then looked him up and down with open appreciation. "You look great, as usual. Addie and your grandpa come in all the time, but I never see you," Tina continued. "I'm glad you were able to make it by." She turned to Delaney. "I'm Tina Johnson."

"Dee." Delaney clasped Tina's hand in a firm shake.

"Nice to meet you." Tina smiled broadly, winking at Corbin. "Is she your girlfriend?"

"Yes," he said matter-of-factly.

"She's a beauty. I would've expected nothing less from you." She motioned to the empty waiting room as she went back to her desk and picked up the handset of her phone. "Have a seat, and I'll let the nurses know you're here."

"Addie's meeting us," Corbin said.

Tina nodded. "Sounds good." No sooner had she spoken the words than Addie came through the double glass doors.

"Hey, Tina," she said, flashing a smile. Then she saw Delaney and Corbin in the waiting room. She went to them, giving each a hug. Her eyes stopped at Corbin.

"You okay?"

Delaney looked at him, realizing he'd gone pale.

He nodded, his teeth clenched so tight a marble had formed in the corner of his jaw.

"It'll be all right," Delaney said giving him a reassuring smile as she touched his arm. He seemed to relax a fraction at her touch.

A nurse in her early twenties opened the side door. "Hi, I'm Judy. Come on back," she said with a brisk smile. "You came at a good time," she said, looking back at them over her shoulder as they followed her down the hall. "Miss Lou Ella's awake."

When they reached the room, Addie walked right in, but Corbin paused at the threshold. Delaney could feel the inner turmoil churning inside him, almost as though it were her own. She saw the flash of panic in his eyes. "You can do this." She willed him to look at her. "I'll be right beside you."

He took in a deep breath, nodding.

"Look who came to see you," Addie said in a high-pitched voice a volume too loud.

Delaney stepped into the room practically pulling Corbin with her. Her heart sank when she saw the frail woman lying in the bed. Lou Ella was a waif, probably not weighing a hundred pounds. Her silver hair was short, but so thin on top that only a few wisps covered her scalp. She turned to look at them, a blank expression on her face.

"It's me and Corbin, Gram," Addie said kindly.

Lou Ella clutched her nightgown. Her splotched, leathery skin was so paper-thin that the veins under her hand looked like a blue rake. Delaney looked at Corbin who had tears running down his cheeks. Tentatively, he moved to her bedside.

"Gram," he uttered.

Tears bubbled from Addie's eyes as she smiled. "I think she's happy to see you. You should talk to her."

Delaney stayed close to Corbin's side.

"This is my girlfriend, Delaney," Corbin said.

Delaney caught the look of surprise on Addie's face, realized Corbin had called her Delaney again, instead of Dee. But it was better to let that slide right now.

"Hi, Lou Ella," Delaney said softly. "Wallace told me what a remarkable woman you are." Her voice hitched. "I know he was right because I can see how much your grandchildren love you."

Lou Ella's lower lip started working as she wound a hand around her nightgown. She seemed to be concentrating, like she was trying to remember something. "Applesauce," she croaked.

"Do you want applesauce?" Addie asked, looking at Judy who was standing in the corner, as if to give them plenty of space and yet still be close enough to offer assistance if needed.

Judy stepped up. "Miss Lou Ella had applesauce this morning for breakfast, didn't you?" She went to the bed and adjusted the pillows behind Lou Ella's back. "Let's help you sit up, so you can visit."

"No," Lou Ella cried out in annoyance, pushing Judy.

Delaney flinched, the outburst taking her by surprise. She looked at Corbin, could tell he was trying to hold it together. She rubbed her hand up and down his arm, hoping it would help soothe him.

"Now, Lou Ella," Judy began in a cheerful tone. "Don't hit." She looked around the room, meeting everyone's eyes. "She gets excited when she has visitors. Just give her a second to adjust." She stepped back against the wall.

"I'm sorry." Corbin's voice grew strangled as he gulped and tried again. "I'm sorry I haven't been here for you." He looked at Addie. "I'm sorry I left you holding the bag." Long pause. His shoulders shook. "I just couldn't stand to see her like this."

"I know," Addie said, tears falling freely down her cheeks. She smiled slightly. "We all just get through it the best we can." She turned to Lou Ella. "Gram, Corbin came to see you."

Corbin stepped forward and ever so gently placed a hand over Lou Ella's. For a second, it looked like she might yank her hand away. But instead she peered intently into Corbin's face like she was searching for something. For an instant, the cloudiness in her eyes parted. Her mouth formed the word, a whisper of sound issuing out. "Cor—"

"She knows," Addie said, putting a hand over her heart. She laughed and cried at the same time. "She knows you're here."

In the next second, Lou Ella's expression changed, going to anger, then fear as she jerked her hand from underneath Corbin's. "Go away!" she yelled, pushing his arm with surprising strength.

Judy stepped up. "Now, Miss Lou Ella. Be nice," she said in a soothing voice, like she was speaking to a child. She offered Corbin an apologetic smile. "I'm sorry, but the heavy drugs make her irritable."

Corbin frowned. "Heavy drugs?"

"For the pain," Judy explained. "The doctors keep Miss Lou Ella sedated most of the time."

Fury flashed in Corbin's eyes as he glared at Judy. "So they won't have to deal with her outbursts?"

She gave him a funny look. "No, because of the brain cancer."

The only sound in the room was the ragged intake of Corbin's breath. His knees buckled as he caught hold of the metal footboard on the bed for support. He looked at Addie through crazed eyes. "Gram has brain cancer?"

"Pops and I didn't know how to tell you," she stammered. "That's why we wanted you to come here ... to find a way to tell her goodbye." She looked to Delaney for help, but Delaney could only shake her head.

Corbin's face turned a shade darker, his eyes blazing. Delaney shrank back, afraid he might punch something.

Instead he straightened his shoulders and balled his fists. "Let's go!" he roared, turning on his heel and storming out. Delaney looked at Addie who spread her hands in defeat, then rushed to catch up with him.

20

Corbin raised the axe and brought it down full force, the blade slicing into the dense wood of the chopping block. He pulled the blade free and raised the axe high, bringing it down again. Curses flew from his mouth, his mind on fire as he hit the block again and again. Tears mixed with his rage as he used every last bit of strength he possessed to obliterate the block. It was so utterly unfair! Not only was Gram robbed of her mind, but now she was dying. And Pops and Addie hadn't told him. What would've happened if he hadn't come home? Would they have waited until Gram passed to tell him she had cancer?

When his anger was spent, he dropped the axe blade to the ground, keeping hold of the handle. His shoulders slumped, his breaths came in short bursts, sending puffs of steam into the air. After they left the care center, Delaney had tried to offer comfort, but he barely heard a word as he sped back to the cabin where he'd jumped out and grabbed the axe.

He glanced at the cabin and realized with a start that Delaney was pressed against the window, watching him. The stricken expression on her face said it all. His blood ran cold as the knowledge pricked him like a thousand needles all at once. Delaney was afraid of his anger ... afraid of him. When she realized he'd seen her, she stepped back, the lace curtain falling over her face. Shame covered him, giving way to a numb coldness that touched every speck of his body. He'd lost himself in the scorching river of anger that raged through him, giving no thought to how this might look to Delaney who was ultra-sensitive about violence, considering her background.

He breathed out a heavy sigh as he put the axe away and trudged up the steps. When he opened the door, his eye caught on Delaney sitting on the couch, her hands clasped tightly, a pinched expression on her tear-stained face.

He ran both hands through his hair, feeling like an idiot. He removed his coat and put it on the rack before going to her side. He sat down beside her. "I'm sorry," he began, touching her arm.

She whirled around to face him. "Don't!" Tears pooled in her eyes, her lower lip quivering. "I thought you were different."

The accusation mixed with hurt in her eyes made him want to crawl under the couch. "I am different." The fact that she kept comparing him to Tuck Allen was insulting. How could she think he was like that monster?

A hard laugh gurgled in her throat. "Clearly."

"Look, I was upset. The news about Gram threw me for a loop."

"I can understand you being upset ... angry." She shuddered. "But what I can't tolerate is violence."

His voice rose, the anger resurfacing. "Because I pounded a chopping block?" His eyes narrowed. "Everyone gets upset, Delaney."

She hugged her arms. "But not everyone goes berserk." Her dark eyes filled with fear. "I can't go through that again."

His jaw tightened. "Through what? I'm not a robot. I have feelings." His voice broke. "I just found out that my grandmother's dying. Cut me a little slack here."

She bit her lower lip to stay the trembling. For a second, they sat looking at each other until she finally spoke. "I'm sorry about your grandmother. I truly am. But I can't be with someone who's so ... angry."

He rattled off a hard laugh. Yeah, he was angry, so furious that it was roasting him from the inside out. "Just because I'm angry doesn't mean that I'd ever hurt you."

Tears slipped from her eyes and rolled down her cheeks. "I'm sorry," she croaked. "But this isn't gonna work."

Corbin couldn't believe what he was hearing. She was giving up on him so soon? Before they even had a chance to get started, just because he'd gotten mad and pulverized a chopping block? "I love you," he said quietly. "Does that mean anything to you?"

The door opened. Pops' eyes rounded as he looked at the two of them. "Is everything all right?"

Delaney hiccuped with emotion, her hand going over her mouth. "Excuse me." She got up and fled the room.

A look of concern washed over Pops. "What was that all about?"

Corbin gave him a hard look. "Why didn't you tell me about Gram? The brain cancer?"

Pops blinked a couple times, rubbing a hand over his jaw. "I tried yesterday."

"What?" Corbin flung back.

Pops sat down in the recliner. "I tried to tell you," he began, "but you wouldn't listen."

"You should've told me earlier."

"Earlier?" Pops chuckled dryly. "I couldn't even get you to come home for a visit, how was I supposed to tell you that?"

"You could've called."

Pops' eyebrow shot up. "And have you self-destruct?"

He rocked back. "I hardly think I'd self-destruct," he muttered.

"Look, it's been hard enough for you to come to terms with Lou Ella being put in the care center." He paused. "I didn't want to add insult to injury."

Acid rose in his throat. "You should've told me." He shot Pops a condemning look.

"I'm not the enemy here, son." Tears gathered in his eyes. "You don't think it's been hard for me? To sit by helplessly, watching my sweetheart deteriorate? First her mind? Then her body? I love her with all my heart."

"I love her too." A sob rose in Corbin's chest. "I know it's not your fault. It's my fault. I couldn't come back ... couldn't face it." This time, he was unable to stop the tears.

"It's nobody's fault." Pops was at his side in two steps. He sat down and put his arms around Corbin, letting the grief flow out.

DELANEY PULLED her knees into her chest and wrapped her arms around them, staring unseeingly ahead. Her life was a tangled mess. Maybe she'd overreacted. But watching Corbin strike the chopping block over and over, his face twisted in rage, had jolted her to the core. How many times had she seen that same ruthless look on Tuck's face before he vented his anger on her? She shuddered, her stomach churning. Would she ever be whole again? Free from the fear? While her rational mind knew that it wasn't fair to project Tuck's sins on Corbin, her feelings screamed otherwise.

A knock sounded at the door.

"Go away," she said reflexively. She'd have to face Corbin sooner or later, figure out if her reaction to his anger was valid or not. But for now, she just wanted to be left alone.

Another knock.

She gritted her teeth. "I said go away!" Why couldn't Corbin allow her some time to sort this through?

"It's Wallace."

She jerked, heat stinging her cheeks. "Oh, sorry." Hastily, she wiped her tears with her palms.

"Can I come in?"

She didn't want to see anyone right now, not even Wallace. But she didn't want to be rude. She blew out a long breath. "Sure."

As he came in, she smoothed down her shirt and sat up, trying not to dwell on how horrible she must look.

Wallace sat down on the edge of the bed.

She frowned. "Did Corbin send you in here to talk to me?" It wasn't right for Corbin to make his grandfather do his dirty work. If Corbin wanted to talk to her, he needed to face her himself.

"No, he doesn't even realize I'm in here."

"Really?" She eyed him to see if he was telling the truth.

"Corbin went out."

She stiffened. "Where?"

"To grab a pizza for dinner." He paused. "And I suspect to apologize to Addie for the way he reacted to Lou Ella's cancer."

"Oh." At least Corbin had the decency to apologize for being wrong. This made her feel a little better about him, and somewhat guilty for jumping the gun.

Wallace gave her a tentative look. "Corbin told me what happened with the chopping block."

She went to rub her hand through her hair, realized the wig was there, so she touched it instead. "You're probably thinking I'm nuts for getting so upset."

"No, not at all."

"Really?" The kindness in his eyes caused a lump to form in her throat.

"After what you've been through, it's understandable that you're upset."

She hugged her arms to ward off a shiver. "I've been trying to take your advice, to feed the right wolf ..." she paused "... but it's hard." She let out a nervous laugh. "That other wolf's not going down quietly, I can tell you that." Wallace's analogy had given her hope that she could change, could vanquish the old fears and start fresh. But now she wondered if it was only a pipe dream.

"Be patient with yourself. It takes time to reshape your thoughts. But with persistence, patience, and a whole lot of prayer, it'll happen."

More tears. Ugh! She felt like such a crybaby. "I dunno." She looked away, unable to face his probing gaze.

"Delaney."

She was surprised that he'd called her Delaney. "Yes?"

"Corbin cares about you and you care about him. Don't let fear keep you apart from him."

"I can't be with a man who can't control his anger."

Wallace laughed. "Then you're out of luck."

"What?" Not the answer she was expecting.

"All men experience anger, frustration. It's how we're wired. Men have to be warriors to take care of their families." He looked her in the eye. "The thing you fear most about Corbin is also what makes him great ... what draws you to him."

She grumbled out a laugh. "Tell me about it. I've always been attracted to the wrong sort of man."

He arched an eyebrow. "If you're including Corbin in that list, then I'm afraid I'm going to have to disagree with you."

She just looked at him, at a loss for words.

"Sure Corbin's impetuous, even reckless at times, but he has a heart of gold." His eyes went moist. "Which is why this thing with his grandmother's tearing him up inside." He gave her a perceptive look. "It's why whatever happened to him in the military still haunts him."

The words burned into Delaney's breast with a conviction that surprised her. Corbin was good in all the areas that counted.

"Corbin has a temper. He'll get mad and beat some inanimate object to a pulp, but he would never hurt you." His eyes held hers. "In fact, his burning desire to keep you safe may be the thing that does you both in."

She frowned. "I don't understand."

"I hope I'm not speaking out of turn here, but I think Corbin's making a big mistake."

She leaned forward waiting for him to expound. "What do you mean?" she asked when he remained silent.

He cocked his head like he was gathering his thoughts. "The best way I can describe it is to tell you what happened to me once. I was with a group of fellow hunters, tracking a grizzly bear that had mauled a hiker. We tracked the bear for twenty or so miles through the forest before we caught a glimpse of him. One of my buddies shot him several times. The grizzly kept going, but we knew he'd been hit because of the trail of blood spots."

"It was getting dark. Half the men wanted to go after the bear and put an end to the chase. But the other half was tired, wanted to set up camp and wait until daylight to track him. After a few rounds of arguments, the latter group won. We found a place by a stream and set up camp for the night. About two in the morning, when everyone was asleep, the enraged grizzly charged into the camp. As we were scrambling for cover and to get our rifles, the bear killed three men and injured several others before we could put it down." He paused. "Had we gone after the bear, lives would've been saved." Intensity burned in Wallace's eyes. "No matter how long you run, Hugh Allen's going to eventually find you."

A shiver slithered down Delaney's spine. Wallace was right. There was no way they could evade Hugh forever.

"You can't change that," Wallace continued, "but what you can change is how and when he comes."

Horror trickled over her as she caught the meaning of his words. "Are you saying we should lure him here?" The thought of doing so had her quaking.

Wallace's jaw tightened. "That's exactly what I'm saying. Bring him to our territory where we'll be waiting. That's the only hope you have of outsmarting him."

"Have you told this to Corbin?"

His brows furrowed in frustration. "Yes."

Her mind whirled, trying to decide if Wallace was right. "What did he say?"

"Corbin won't even entertain the idea because he wants so desperately to keep you safe. But like I said, while his intentions are noble, it will be to your detriment in the end. Think of how much better off me and my hunting buddies would've been had the bear not caught us unaware."

"Why're you telling me this?"

"Because Corbin loves you too much to voluntarily put you in danger."

Her mind caught on the word *love*, running it through her head a few times. *I love him too.* The thought caused her to jerk slightly. She shook her head, putting her focus back on the problem at hand. "What do you want me to do?"

A grim smile spread over Wallace's lips. "To be the bait. Lure the grizzly here to our trap."

She sucked in a breath, fear settling like stone in her gut. Could she do it? Be brave enough to face this? Or was luring Hugh Allen here utter stupidity? She bit her lower lip, trying to decide the best course of action. "I'll have to give it some thought," she finally said.

Wallace nodded. "Fair enough. But don't let it sit too long because my gut tells me we're running out of time."

She went cold all over, the knowledge settling into her like the march of doom. Somehow, in a way she couldn't explain, she knew that Wallace was right. Their time was almost up.

21

When Corbin returned to the cabin after visiting with Addie and picking up pizza, he figured he'd find Delaney locked in her room. He was shocked when he walked through the door and found Delaney and Pops playing a game of checkers.

"Crown me," Delaney said triumphantly, as she pushed her red checker into the back row of Pops' side of the board.

Pops groaned. "Not again. At the rate you're getting kinged, it's bound to be a short game."

Delaney let out a light laugh that tingled through Corbin's senses, shooting rays of hope into his heart. Maybe things would be okay between him and Delaney. He was sorry he lost his temper and vented it on the chopping block, but he couldn't walk on eggshells around her 24/7.

Corbin placed the pizza on the table. "Who's hungry?"

"I'm starved," Delaney said.

Corbin was glad to see she had an appetite. That was a good sign that her emotional state had improved.

"Let's pause our game and continue it tomorrow," Pops said with a sly grin. "I'm not overly anxious to get whupped tonight."

Delaney laughed again, shaking her head. She cast a surreptitious glance at Corbin and he could tell she was nervous. They needed to have a conversation to clear the air, but it would have to wait until after dinner.

Corbin retrieved three glasses from the cabinet and reached for the two-liter bottle of soda. Then he grabbed three plates.

Pops walked to the coatrack and reached for his jacket.

"You're not staying for dinner?" Corbin asked, hoping he wasn't so he could work things out with Delaney in private.

"No, I need to get home." He winked. "And three's a crowd."

A deep blush came over Delaney's face making her look so beautiful that Corbin nearly lost his breath. He was falling hard for this woman, but could they work through their problems? If not, he was headed for a major heartbreak. "I'll see you tomorrow, Pops."

He nodded.

Corbin felt closer to Pops tonight than he had in years. The two of them had a breakthrough of sorts earlier. Corbin was still torn up about Gram's condition, but he no longer blamed the situation on Pops or Addie. Truthfully, he never had. It was just an excuse to hold his own guilt at bay. Seeing Gram, realizing how bad off she was, there was no way Pops could take care of her at home. Corbin and Addie had a quick but meaningful conversation where he told her how much he appreciated everything she'd done for their grandparents. It was good to bury the hatchet and mend his family relationships. Now he hoped to do the same with Delaney.

After Pops left, they sat down at the table. Suddenly, Corbin was nervous, unsure what to say. Delaney cleared her throat when he reached for a slice of pizza. He froze mid-action. "What?"

She gave him a censuring look, but there was a hint of amusement in her eyes, which were silky pools of chocolate tonight. "The prayer."

"Oh, yeah." Heat crawled up his neck. "Would you like me to say it?"

"Please."

Religion had always been a key element of Corbin's growing up years, so he was well-versed in how to pray. There were times when he hadn't been as consistent with his prayers, particularly after the ordeal in the Philippines when his anger and heartache had nearly consumed him. Nevertheless, he had a strong belief in God and was glad Delaney did too. He started his prayer by expressing gratitude for the food and that they'd been kept safe. Then he asked for continued protection to see them through the ordeal with Hugh Allen. Pushing back emotion, he gave thanks for Gram and asked that she be blessed to have very little pain. He added that he was grateful for her long, fruitful life and the many lives she'd touched, including his. Lastly, he expressed gratitude for Delaney and asked that she be given added peace. When he said *Amen* and opened his eyes, he noticed that Delaney had tears in her eyes. "Are you okay?"

She smiled slightly, nodding. "Yeah. That was a beautiful prayer. Thank you." He was surprised when she reached for his hand. "I'm sorry I freaked out earlier."

His heart melted a little. "I'm sorry I acted like a buffoon and took my anger out on the chopping block."

"It's okay," she shrugged.

He searched her face. "If you didn't know it by now, I have a temper. I'm working on getting it under control, but it comes out from time to time."

Her eyes lit with laughter, turning them a warm caramel. "You?" she asked in mock astonishment. "No." She pursed her lips. "Come to think of it, I might've guessed that when you laid out my three-hundred-pound bodyguard in the middle of a party."

"Not one of my finer achievements," he said dryly. He looked her in the eye. She was so beautiful—strong, yet vulnerable. And in the short time they'd been together, she was consuming him body and soul. "I know I'm a hothead, but you need to know that I would never hurt you. I love you."

Tears slipped from her eyes. "You're a good man, Corbin Spencer. I know you'd never hurt me." She took in a deep breath. "I'm just trying to fight those demons." She laughed remorsefully. "It's hard, you know?"

"Yes, I do know. We'll fight our demons together. Okay?" He held his breath, awaiting her answer.

"Okay."

He breathed a sigh of relief, knowing they could move forward. Yeah, it would be awesome to know that Delaney loved him too, but it was early in their relationship. Like Pops said, he needed to be patient, give her time. He released her hands. "I guess we should eat the pizza, before it gets cold."

"It looks delicious. I'm glad you got a supreme. It's my favorite."

He smiled. "Another thing we have in common."

She chuckled. "The list is stacking up." She took a large bite. "Very good," she said, a minute later. She reached for her napkin, dabbing her lips. "Oh, I was thinking about the sweetheart dance tomorrow night. I think we should go."

He nearly choked on his pizza. "What?"

"It would mean a lot to Addie ..." She gave him a hopeful look. "And I'd like to dance with you."

Delaney was full of wonderful surprises. His eyes caressed hers, his voice going husky. "We could dance together tonight, here in the cabin. In front of a warm fire." The very thought of dancing with Delaney, holding her close, swaying to soft music, swirled anticipation through his veins.

Color seeped into her cheeks. "Yeah, we could," she said evasively. "But it would mean a lot to Addie for us to go to the dance. And I'd like to get dressed up and go out on the town."

Absolutely not. "What if someone recognizes you? Madison came close at the lodge. We can't take another risk."

"Madison came close, but she didn't recognize me." She touched her hair. "You have to admit, I look so different with this thing on."

"True," he conceded, "but do you really think we should chance it?"

"I think it'll be okay." Her eyes pled with his. "The lights will be low. I'll wear extra makeup. Will you take me to the sweetheart dance? Please?"

Why was she being so stubborn? He crossed his hands over his chest. "No."

Irritation flashed in her eyes as she squared her jaw. "Fine. If you won't take me, then I'll go by myself."

"Have you lost your mind? You really want me to take you to a place packed with people?"

She looked him in the eye. "I want to get dressed up. Go someplace as a couple. Forget about our problems for a few hours." Her voice quivered slightly. "Is that too much to ask?"

He sighed, knowing how this would end—the same way things had gone down when Gram wanted something from Pops. Eventually, Pops would always give her whatever she wanted. As kids, Corbin and Addie used to joke that Gram had Pops wrapped around her little finger. But for the first time, Corbin understood the situation. How could he say no to a woman like Delaney? From the first moment he saw her, all his thoughts had revolved around making her happy. "Okay, I'll take you."

She rewarded him with a dazzling smile. "Thank you."

"For the record, I still think this is a bad idea."

"Duly noted." She looked at him with an adoring expression. "I hope you know how much I appreciate this."

He softened. "What're you going to wear?"

"My red dress, the one I wore for Sutton's party." She frowned, touching the wig. "I hope it looks okay with this hair color. Do you think the reds will clash?"

"I think you'll look stunning no matter what you wear," he said sincerely.

"Thanks," she murmured in appreciation, her thick lashes brushing her cheekbones as she lowered her eyes to her plate. The movement was subtle, yet so distinctly feminine, making Corbin want to jump up and pull her into his arms this very minute. No, better at least wait until they'd had a chance to eat dinner.

He thought of something. He didn't have any formal clothes except for the white tux, stained with Anton's blood from the fight. He'd have to take it to the cleaners first thing in the morning, see if they could do a rush job, and make it look decent enough to wear. He thought of his upcoming phone call to Sutton this evening. Maybe it was better not to mention that he was taking Delaney to a public dance. Sutton wouldn't approve, too much risk of exposure. While they were at the dance, Corbin would have to do his best to make sure the two of them stayed out of the limelight. He glanced at Delaney. Who was he kidding? A woman like her could never be kept in the shadows. Even with the wig, she was a walking bombshell.

Last night during their phone call, Sutton mentioned the possibility of surrounding Hugh and his men in Northern Cal and putting a stop to this whole business. Corbin was all for that, as he'd wanted to hunt Hugh down from the start. According to Sutton, his team on the ground was doing a little more research to make sure they covered all the angles before Sutton made a final decision. Corbin made a mental note to ask Sutton about it tonight. If the threat were removed in the next twenty-four hours, the dance would be a non-issue. That would be the best solution. A long shot perhaps, but it was something to hope for.

"Are you okay?"

He forced a smile. "Yeah, why?"

Delaney studied him. "You had a funny look on your face."

It was uncanny how perceptive she was at picking up on his feelings. "I was just lamenting my lack of dancing skills."

She laughed. "Is that right?"

"Yep."

Her eyes sparkled. "Well, I guess I'll have to teach you a few steps ..." her gaze moved over him in that slow sultry way that sizzled his blood "... for practice sake."

A smile broke over his lips. "I'm all about the practice."

22

The Bear Claw Resort was brimming with people. Corbin placed his hand on the small of Delaney's back, maneuvering her through the crowd as he nodded at familiar faces.

A guy stepped in front of them, wearing a large smile. "Hey, buddy, I didn't know you were back in town." He gave Corbin's hand a hearty shake.

Scott Linton and Corbin played high school football together. Corbin hadn't seen Scott in several years, might not have recognized him out of context. Gangly in high school, Scott had put on at least fifty pounds.

"Good to see you, Scott."

"Yeah, you too, man." He turned to Delaney. "Who's the babe?"

Babe? Seriously? Scott was certainly lacking in the manners department. "This is my girlfriend, Dee," Corbin said coolly.

"Nice to meet you," Delaney clipped, picking up on Corbin's annoyance.

Scott didn't try to hide his appreciation as he looked her up and down. "You're certainly elevating the class here tonight."

"Thanks," Delaney said with a surprised laugh.

Corbin saw Addie across the room, a welcome distraction. "Take care. We're going over to say hello to my sister."

Scott nodded, stepping back to let them by. They pushed past him. "Good to see you," Scott called after them.

Addie broke into a smile when she saw them. "I'm so glad you came." She hugged Delaney first, then Corbin. "You both look fantastic."

"Thanks," they said simultaneously. They turned the same direction as Addie, their backs against the wall, facing the crowd.

A wicked light came into Addie's eye as she gave Corbin the once-over. She turned to Delaney. "What I want to know is how in the heck did you convince my brother to wear a tux?"

Corbin chuckled. "Because Dee has the art of persuasion down to a science, that's how."

Delaney's eyebrow shot up. "Really?"

"Yes, really," he countered, placing his arm around her waist, drawing her close. "I believe someone promised me a dance," he murmured in her ear.

She turned and looked up into his eyes. "It would be my pleasure."

"Excuse us, Addie," he said, sweeping Delaney into his arms and pulling her onto the dance floor. He loved having Delaney this close, marveled at how petite she was. She was an excellent dancer, moving in perfect step with him. Despite his misgivings about safety, he was suddenly glad they'd come. If all was going according to plan, Sutton and his guys were moving in on Hugh right about now. Hopefully, by the time Corbin and Delaney returned to the cabin, it would all be over. Corbin had been tempted to tell Delaney all that was happening, but didn't want to cause her additional stress. It was better to let things unfold, then tell her when it was over.

He pulled her closer, then leaned in and nuzzled her ear. "You're so beautiful," he uttered. He lowered his mouth to her earlobe, planting a light string of kisses down her slender neck. She melted into him, resting her head on his shoulder. The song ended all too soon. Corbin hoped the band would play another slow song, but they played a fast one instead. Delaney pulled away from him. "Do you wanna dance to this one?" He wasn't in the mood to fast-dance, but would if Delaney wanted to.

She shrugged. "We could ... or we could go back and talk to Addie."

"Let's catch up with Addie," he said quickly. They walked to where they'd last been standing, but Addie wasn't there. Delaney pointed. "She's dancing."

Corbin spotted Addie with a tall, dark-haired guy that he'd never seen before. Her smile was a mile wide, and she was dancing her heart out. She waved when she realized they were watching her.

"Your sister's spunky," Delaney said admiringly.

"Yes, she is," Corbin chuckled.

"She looks very pretty in her blue dress."

Did she? Corbin looked. Yes, Addie did look good. Corbin had been too consumed with Delaney's fantastic looks to pay attention to anyone else.

"Well, well, didn't expect to see you here tonight," a deep voice rumbled.

Corbin turned as Sheriff Cliff Hendricks approached. The old sheriff had gone gray and developed a paunch since Corbin had last seen him, but he still wore the same disapproving scowl Corbin remembered.

The Sheriff's bushy brows bunched. "What're you doing here, Spencer?"

The hair on Corbin's neck stood. There had never been any love lost between him and Sheriff Hendricks. In the Sheriff's eyes, Corbin had always been a loser. "Hello, Cliff."

Sheriff Hendricks frowned like he didn't appreciate Corbin using his first name. He looked at Delaney. "Who are you?" he asked bluntly.

Delaney arched an eyebrow, her eyes sparking. "The name's Dee," she shot back. "And who might you be?"

Corbin laughed inwardly when the man's face went red. It had taken all of two seconds for Delaney to put the old geezer in his place.

"I'm the sheriff," he blustered.

She didn't back down an inch. "Do you have a name?"

He blinked rapidly. "Uh, Cliff Hendricks."

"Nice to meet you, Cliff," she said.

The sheriff turned to Corbin, his eyes narrowing. "I don't want you causing any trouble."

Irritation scorched through Corbin. He tried to think of a rebuttal, but Delaney reacted first.

She laughed lightly. "Are you always this friendly to guests? Corbin told me how nice the people of Birchwood Springs were, but he might have to retract that statement."

The sheriff's eyes bulged.

"From where I'm standing, the only one causing trouble is you," she continued. "We were minding our own business until you came up." She flashed a cheery smile. "If you'll excuse us, we were going to get some punch. It was nice meeting you, Cliff." She let her voice hang a little on his name as she lifted her chin in the air and walked regally towards the refreshment table. It was all Corbin could do not to hoot in the old sheriff's face, as he hurried to catch up with her.

"Wow, that was incredible. You cut ole Cliff down to size. I would give anything to have that on video."

She didn't stop walking until they reached the table. When she turned, he realized she was livid. "That man was intolerable," she hissed.

"Yes, he is."

She shook her head. "What's his problem?"

"Cliff's always been a pompous jerk. He got it in for me when I soaped up the fountains in front of the bank where his wife worked."

A laugh gurgled in her throat. "Are you serious?"

"Yep. And then there was the time he caught me sneaking into this very ski resort."

She shook her head. "You were a menace."

He drew his lips together. "I'm afraid so." A smile tugged at his lips. "But I'm a changed man now."

She put a hand on her hip. "Try telling that to the poor chopping block you destroyed."

He winced. "I guess I deserved that."

She cocked her head like she'd just thought of something. "It must've been hard to come back here, when people like the sheriff have so little regard for you."

"Yeah, I suppose. But coming back has made me realize that for every person like Sheriff Hendricks there are lots of good people too." His eyes held hers. "The main reason I brought you here was because I knew I could keep you safe." *Of course coming to a public party wasn't part of the plan, but so far, everything seems to be going okay.*

She gave him a radiant smile. "Thank you."

"For what?"

She touched his cheek. "For being you."

A few minutes later, after they'd gotten their fill of punch and cookies, Delaney motioned at the stage. "Who's the band?"

"I dunno. Someone local, I guess. I've never heard of them before."

She pursed her lips. "They're pretty good."

He made a face. "I would hardly call singing off key and fumbling over the lyrics *good*."

She laughed. "Don't be mean." She motioned with her head. "Let's get closer, watch them perform."

"Ah, the truth comes out. You're wishing you were up there performing. It's hard to be a peon in the audience," he teased, "after you've gotten a taste of stardom. Don't worry, you'll be back up there before you know it."

She rolled her eyes. "Whatever." She tugged on his hand. "Come on."

DELANEY'S NERVES were jumping like a scared rabbit. Had they not been in a crowded place, she was sure Corbin would've picked up on her emotional state by now. Wallace's bear story kept running through her mind. He was right. Time was running out, she could feel it. But she didn't want to do anything to harm Corbin or his family. Wallace assured her that everything would be okay, but what if he was mistaken? He'd never met Hugh, didn't realize how ruthless Hugh was. Still, it would be better to face Hugh when they were prepared. He would find them eventually. She offered up a silent prayer, asking for courage to do what must be done.

They were standing near the stage, watching the band. Corbin was right. The group of middle-aged men weren't very good, but the audience didn't seem to mind. Corbin's arm was draped over her shoulders as they swayed to the beat of the music.

"Hey there," Madison Wells chirped loudly as she threaded through the people to reach their side.

Delaney cringed. *Not that dreadful woman again.*

"Hey, Madison," Corbin said dully. The pained look on his face was so obvious that Delaney couldn't help but chuckle.

Madison gave her a blistering look. "What's so funny?"

"Oh, nothing," Delaney said nonchalantly. *Just wondering when you're gonna get a clue that Corbin is taken,* she added mentally.

"Remember when we came to a sweetheart dance together, Corbin?" Madison asked, her tone going intimate. "It was right here on this very floor. We danced every dance and then afterwards, we went back to my house." Her eyes took on a dreamy look. "You played the guitar and sang that song you wrote for me. Then we got into the hot tub together." She giggled. "Well, I'm sure I don't need to remind you about that. It's certainly imprinted on my mind and heart."

Hot needles rained down on Delaney as she looked at Corbin's strangled expression. Then she saw the look of triumph on Madison's face.

It took every ounce of control she could muster to keep from clocking the idiotic woman.

Time to act, her mind screamed. At the same moment, Corbin cleared his throat like he was trying to come up with something to say that would smooth things over. Before she could talk herself out of it, Delaney took off the wig, her hair tumbling around her shoulders. Tonight, she'd left off the hairnet and fixed the wig loosely on her head for this very purpose.

Madison's eyes bugged as Corbin's narrowed.

"You're Delaney Mitchell," Madison stammered.

She threw back her head, tossing a hand through her hair. "In the flesh," she said loudly.

"What're you doing?" Corbin muttered.

Before he could grab her arm, she rushed forward and climbed onto the stage. The music dribbled off as the musicians stopped playing one by one, gaping at her like she was a ghost. Murmurs rustled through the crowd. She smiled brightly, stepping up to the lead singer. "May I?"

"Of course." He gave her an enamored grin as he handed her the microphone and stepped back.

Showtime. "Good evening, Birchwood Springs!" she boomed. "It's a pleasure to be here with you tonight."

Thunderous applause rippled through the audience. "It's Delaney Mitchell," a man yelled.

"I'd like to sing one of my favorites, a song about my home state of Alabama." She looked at the man holding the guitar. "May I?"

"Of course," he said proudly, removing the strap and handing it to her.

Delaney could only imagine what Corbin must be thinking, but she was doing what had to be done. She started playing and singing. The band joined in shortly. She was only halfway through the song when she saw Corbin striding towards her, a furious expression on his handsome face.

He took her arm. "Let's go," he hissed in her ear.

She jerked out of his grasp, continuing the song.

"I said, let's go," he repeated.

Before she could protest, he put his arms around her waist and threw her over his shoulder, the guitar falling noisily to the floor. Boos rang out across the audience as he carried her offstage.

"Put me down," she demanded, beating his shoulders and kicking. He paid her no mind, carrying her through the backstage area and out the exit door. Of all the humiliating things to do! "I said put me down!" she screamed.

Finally, he did so, dropping her on the ground where she landed square on her rear end. "Ouch," she yelped.

He ran both hands through his hair, a look of disbelief on his face. He pointed at the resort "What was that all about? Are you trying to get yourself killed?"

She jumped to her feet. "On the contrary, I'm trying to save us."

"How? By letting the whole world know where you are?"

"By luring the bear to us."

The whites of his eyes popped. "What?"

"Wallace told me the story about the bear and how people got killed because it attacked when they were unaware."

He barked out an incredulous laugh. "Are you talking about that stupid bear story Pops tells?"

She rocked back. "Yeah, but it wasn't a story. It really happened to him and his hunting buddies."

He shook his head in disgust. "Yeah, it happened, but the story gets bigger with the bear growing more ferocious and more people dying every time he tells it."

She gulped in a breath, horror trickling down her spine. "Wallace said that Hugh would eventually find us and that it would be better here, where we can get prepared."

He swore. "The old man's losing it. Oh, my gosh," he lamented. "I can't believe he went behind my back and convinced you to do something so stupid. People in the audience were videoing you, Delaney. It won't take long for the word to get out that you're here."

She jutted out her chin. "I know, that was the point. And it wasn't stupid."

"What?" he fired back.

She straightened her shoulders, looking him in the eye. "It wasn't stupid," she repeated. "Your grandfather's right. We can't keep running. We have to face Hugh. On our own terms, on our own turf. That's the only chance we have." The truth of her words settled into her heart as she spoke them, letting her know she'd made the right decision. "Heaven favors the righteous cause," she said quietly.

"Are you listening to yourself? Hugh's a cold-blooded killer." There was a crazed look on his face.

She balled her fists. "Don't you think I know that?" Her voice rose. She locked eyes with him. "I'm tired of running. We have to end this thing once and for all."

He shook his head, sounding weary and defeated. "I want it to be over too, but at the end of this I want you to still be breathing."

She stepped closer to him. "Look at me."

He grunted.

"I said look at me," she ordered.

Reluctantly, he turned his eyes to hers.

"It'll be okay. Wallace is right. The only way around this thing is to face it head on. I want a life with you, Corbin Spencer." A lump formed in her throat. "I love you."

He blinked in surprise, a tiny smile flickering over his lips. "I can't believe you said it out loud."

She touched his face. "Like I said, I want a life with you, Corbin Spencer. A good, long, fruitful life away from the fear. Do you understand what I'm saying?"

His eyes went soft. "I love you too. And I want that same thing."

"Good, we're in agreement." She squared her jaw. "From this point forward, no more running."

A resolved expression came over him, reminding her how much of a warrior he really was. "No more running," he repeated, a fierce light shining in his eyes.

23

Pieces started falling like dominos when Corbin and Delaney got back to the cabin. Addie came in behind them, demanding to know why Corbin hadn't told her Delaney's real identity. Tears rose in Addie's eyes when Delaney told her all that was happening. She looked at Corbin, fear streaking her expression as she asked. "What're we going to do?"

A second later, Corbin's secure phone buzzed. It was Sutton saying that he'd seen the video of Delaney online. Then he dropped a whammy—a shootout had taken place when his guys tried to capture Hugh. Three of Sutton's guys had been killed, along with the woman posing as Delaney. Hugh had killed her himself, after he found out she wasn't Delaney. Hugh had lost half a dozen men, but probably didn't give it a second thought. Sutton was sure Hugh was on his way to Colorado.

Corbin's gut churned. Pops was a fool. He'd put them all in danger. Sutton was sending a team of guys in a private plane, due to arrive in less than three hours. While that was great, Corbin knew he couldn't trust Delaney's, and now his family's, fate to a group of strangers. There was only one thing he could do. It would require him to eat humble pie, but that was okay. He'd do whatever was necessary.

He punched in a familiar number. *Please answer*, he prayed.

"Hello."

"Zane, hey, it's Corbin."

A pause came over the line.

Corbin tightened his hold on the phone. "You still there?"

"Yeah, just surprised to hear from you."

He swallowed. "I've got a situation here. I'm gonna need your help and the help of SEAL Team 7."

Zane grunted in surprise. "It must be serious if you're calling."

"It's a matter of life and death."

Another pause and then, "All right. I'm listening."

In the matter of a few hours, the cabin was swarming with Sutton's security guys. Delaney could sense the nervousness of the group, oozing like toxins into the air. Corbin told her about the shootings in Northern Cal, how Hugh had killed her double out of spite. Alarm trickled down her spine, sending chills racing over her body. Her throat constricted, making it hard to get a good breath. She put a hand over her chest, willing herself to calm down as she stared at the mindless comedy show blaring on the TV.

Cannon, a former SEAL from Corbin's team, sat down beside her, a friendly smile on his face. "How ya doing?"

"All right," she said, hugging her arms.

There was a hint of faint laughter in his eyes. "That good, huh?"

"Well, as good as a sitting duck can be," she quipped. Why had she listened to Wallace? She was going to die. They all were. Panic sliced through her as she looked at Corbin. He was sitting at the kitchen table, intently talking to Blayze and Zane, two other former members of his SEAL team. Delaney could sense tension between the group and Corbin, knew it was because of what happened in the Philippines. But she could tell Corbin was grateful to have them here.

"It'll be all right," Cannon assured her. "I've been given the personal task of looking after you, and I can assure you, no one will get past me or my weapons."

A laugh gurgled in her throat. Earlier, the former SEAL Team members were teasing Cannon about the arsenal of weapons he carried on his person.

He glanced at the table. "Corbin's been through a lot ... losing his best friend ... and everything else that happened."

"I know."

His eyebrow arched as he turned to her. "How much do you know?"

"All of it. Doug ... the little girl ... how Corbin disobeyed orders."

He let out a low whistle, rubbing a hand over his jaw. "Wow. Corbin told you all of that?"

She nodded, wondering if she should've told him.

"He must really care about you a lot," he mused.

"Yes," she admitted. "And I about him." She paused, wondering if she should say more. The words tumbled from her mouth, almost of their own accord. "For the record, Corbin regrets what happened. And he really appreciates y'all coming to help."

"I'm glad we could be here. River would've come too, but he's on another assignment from Sutton."

"Regardless of how this ends, I want you to know how much I appreciate y'all coming and supporting us." Her voice cracked. "It means a lot."

He offered a reassuring smile. "The Lord is on our side."

Her heart lightened a little. "Yes, I believe that too."

Corbin looked out the window. The first light of dawn was splashing across the hazy sky. Thirty minutes ago, he'd received word from one of Sutton's men that Hugh and his goons had arrived in town. From what they could tell, there were seven of them, including Hugh.

The plan was for Sutton's men to stay on the perimeter of the property and keep watch for Hugh and his men to arrive. Blayze and Addie would go to the care center and watch over Gram while Zane went to Pops' cabin and looked after him. Corbin and Cannon would stay here with Delaney. Sutton's security team would allow Hugh's guys to break the perimeter. As soon as Hugh approached this cabin, Zane and Pops would follow behind them, pinning them in.

Despite the bad blood between them, Corbin was intensely grateful that his former SEAL Team came so quickly to help, proving that no matter what happened in the past they'd always be brothers in the end. Sutton had provided them with bullet-proof vests, radios, and enough artillery to start World War III.

Corbin did a check. "Blayze, how ya doing?"

"All clear here."

"Thor? How about you?"

"Everything's good here." Zane laughed. "Wallace is telling me about the grizzly bear."

"That dumb story's what got us into this mess," Corbin grumbled. "Take everything the old man says with a grain of salt."

"I'll be sure and tell him you said that," Zane teased.

Corbin groaned loudly.

"The man's tough, a real-life Jack Reacher," Zane said, a touch of admiration in his voice.

"Yeah, Pops is tough," Corbin admitted, "but not invincible, contrary to what he believes."

"I hear ya," Zane chortled. "Same goes for all of us, brother."

"Amen." Corbin smiled at the reference. Things were still tense between him and Zane. After all, Zane was the CO of their rescue mission in the Philippines and took it as a personal insult that Corbin defied his orders. But the fact that Zane had rushed to help and brought in the troops, spoke volumes. Corbin vowed then and there that he'd return the favor anytime it was needed.

The radio crackled. He was about to check in on Sutton's guys when he heard shots, followed by shouts. "We're under attack," a man screamed.

"And so it begins," Corbin said under his breath. He looked at Cannon who tightened his hold on his assault rifle.

Delaney's face drained. She was sitting on the floor in front of the couch. *Down low and away from the windows.* "What's happening?" she demanded

"Hugh's here," Corbin said. "His men broke through the perimeter, as planned. Sutton's guys know what to do to make it look real."

She nodded, biting her lower lip.

A series of loud pops sounded through the radio. He heard shattering glass, and explosions bigger than rifles and pistols could make, causing his blood to run cold.

"Take cover!" Zane yelled.

Grenades? Flash bangs? Rocket launchers?

Corbin's heart dropped. Had they underestimated their opponent? "Zane? Are you there? Zane!" he yelled.

Silence.

Corbin clutched his rifle, willing himself to remain calm. Zane was more than capable of handling himself in any situation. He had to hold onto the hope that he and Pops would be okay.

The next five minutes rolled by excruciatingly slow. Relief pelted through him when he heard Zane's voice. "Corbin?"

"You okay?" Corbin yelled into the radio.

"We have a situation," Zane said, his voice tight and controlled.

"Okay." Wariness trickled over Corbin as he glanced at Cannon who also looked concerned.

"Send Delores out if you want your buddy and your grandpa to live," a scratchy voice hissed into the radio.

Delaney let out a cry. "Oh, no." Her hands went to her mouth.

Corbin inched to the window and looked out. A cold sweat broke across his forehead when he saw Zane and Pops standing with their hands up, guns pointed at their backs.

Delaney jumped to her feet, tears welling in her eyes. "I have to go out there," she cried. "He'll kill your friend and Wallace without blinking an eye." A sob wrenched her throat as she wrung her hands. "I was a fool to bring Hugh here."

An image of Doug flashed through Corbin's mind, his lifeless stare, eyes like glass. Then he saw the little girl, heard the mother's shrieks. His throat thickened as he swallowed hard. Corbin sucked in a breath, trying to clear his head. Panic was knocking at the door, and he knew it wouldn't take much for that panic to turn to rage. He locked eyes with Delaney, a feeling of intense love rushing over him. He had to keep her safe, at all costs. *If anyone's going into danger today, it's me.*

Corbin looked out the window to assess the situation. Hugh was standing to the right of Zane, a brazen expression on his face. He was holding the radio in his left hand, a pistol in the right. Two tangos were behind Zane and Pops, pointing guns at their backs. There were two other tangos, one on each side of the gunmen holding Zane and Pops. Five men in all. Had one of Hugh's men been shot? Or was he still lurking around somewhere? What happened to Sutton's men? They should be closing in.

Even as the thought entered his mind, he saw movement behind a tree, realized Sutton's men were here. There were ten of them in all. "Did you see that, Big Gun?" he asked Cannon who was at the other window.

"Yep. Two of Sutton's guys at two o'clock. Another at nine o'clock." Cannon looked at him. "I'm sure the rest are close by. How do you wanna play this?"

"Like we planned in the event of a worst-case scenario." Corbin would go out with his hands up and talk to Hugh. He would walk into the line of fire in an attempt to save those he loved, just as Doug had done. At the word *scumbag*, Cannon and Sutton's men would start firing. Corbin could only hope Zane and Pops didn't get killed in the crossfire. He offered up a silent prayer for their safety. An ironic laugh bubbled in his throat. How many times had he wished to relive the Philippines debacle? *Not like this*, his mind screamed. *Not like this!*

He put down the assault rifle. He had a Glock tucked into the back of his jeans. Another small pistol at his ankle. "You know what to do," he said to Cannon. "Keep her safe."

"Heart of a warrior," Cannon said with a nod.

Delaney's face caved as she rushed into Corbin's arms. "Don't go out there. He'll kill you."

"I'll be all right." He hoped that was the case. But more than anything he had to keep Pops and Zane safe.

"Time's running out!" Hugh yelled. "Ten ... nine ... eight ..."

Corbin cupped her face. "I have to." He had to get out there fast.

"I love you," she uttered.

"I love you too." He pressed his lips to hers.

Hugh's voice rattled through the radio. "Seven ... three ... one." A shot cracked through the air.

Corbin and Delaney both jumped.

A raucous laugh scratched through the radio. Then he swore. "Guess we don't know how to count in Alabama."

Nausea swept over Corbin. He looked at Delaney's stricken expression. Without another word, he stepped through the front door. His heart ripped in two when he saw Pops on the ground. His hand was over his shoulder, blood pooling out.

Fury twisted through Corbin, and instinct made him want to pull out his Glock and start shooting. Then he looked at Zane.

He gave Corbin an imperceptible nod that said, *You've got this.*

It was amazing how much confidence that single look gave Corbin. He held up his hands walking out slowly.

"That's far enough," Hugh said when he got to the bottom of the steps. His cold eyes raked over Corbin. "So you're the one who's been hiding Delores?" His voice was friendly, conversational, a parody of Delaney's more refined Southern accent. "Delores always did like the pretty types. My brother was a pretty boy." A macabre smile twisted over his face. "Better send her out. Or this will end badly."

Corbin glanced at Pops. His face was pale as sand, but he seemed to be hanging in there.

"The Bible says an eye for an eye," Hugh said, a casual lilt in his voice. "Delores has to pay for what she done to my brother."

"What about turning the other cheek?" Corbin demanded, locking eyes with the monster. "Your brother broke into Delaney's house, tried to rape her. He deserved to get shot ... deserved to die."

Hatred flashed in Hugh's eyes, the apathetic mask falling away. "She beguiled my brother!" he screamed.

"Your brother was a wife beater. And you stood back and let it happen."

"Shut up!" Hugh screamed, firing a shot at the ground, a mere foot from where Corbin was standing.

Corbin jumped, his heart going into his throat.

"I said bring her out." Hugh pointed his gun at Pops' chest. "Or the old man gets it!"

DELANEY LOOKED at Cannon who was standing by the window, his body tensed as he waited for the code word. She had to act now while he was preoccupied. Her childhood flashed through her mind. The persistent rumble of her hungry stomach, the filthiness of the trailer, her mother's empty promises that she'd change. Hugh had used the drugs as a means of control, giving her mother a little more each time, until she was totally at his mercy.

It had been a frigid day in February when her mother was buried. In her mind's eye, Delaney felt the swirl of the sleet around her, matching the coldness of her heart. Delaney stood over her mother's coffin and watched it being lowered into the ground. Everything within her wanted vengeance on the man that brought her mother to this point. But she'd been helpless then.

Today, however, there was something she could do. No longer would she stand by and watch Hugh kill the people she loved. A surge of energy spiked through her as she sprang into action. "I'm right here, you scumbag," she yelled, rushing out the door.

"SCUMBAG!" Corbin yelled at the same time Delaney came through the door. Time seemed to slow as he pulled his gun and shot Hugh straight through the heart. His eyes widened in surprise as he went to his knees then fell facedown into the snow. Cannon must've gotten the tango holding a gun on Zane. He fell back. A bullet whizzed past Corbin's right ear as he aimed and took out the tango next to Pops. Zane went down and grabbed the guy's gun that Cannon had shot. At the same time, Sutton's men fired from behind.

It was all over in a matter of seconds. Corbin's first thought was for Delaney. He turned, overjoyed to see her standing, unscathed. A sob wrenched her throat. He looked at Pops, relieved he was okay. Zane was helping Pops to his feet. He, too, was okay.

It was a miracle that they were all alive!

Two of Hugh's men were killed and the other three were being handcuffed by Sutton's men. Delaney stumbled down the steps where she fell into his arms. Cannon came out behind her. "Sorry, I didn't realize she'd gone out until it was too late."

"No worries, my friend. She may be little, but she's stubborn." Corbin pulled her close, rubbing her back. "I'm glad you're okay ... and that it's over."

Delaney pulled away and looked at Hugh's lifeless body, a shudder running through her. "Is he dead?"

"Yes, he's dead."

Her shoulders sagged in relief, tears rolling down her cheeks. "I'm glad it's over."

Corbin looked over as the man next door came outside, a suspicious look on his face. "What's going on here?" he demanded. A look of horror came over him when he saw the dead bodies.

"Nothing you need to be worried about, Gus," Pops said, leaning on Zane for support. "Go back inside."

Gus rushed back in and slammed the door behind him.

"We need to get Wallace to the hospital," Zane said, "before he loses any more blood."

Corbin nodded, noticing that Zane was putting pressure on the wound to stay the bleeding. He left Delaney's side and went to Pops, patting his arm. "You're gonna be okay," he said, his voice hitching. He didn't want to even contemplate how close he came to losing Pops.

"I'll be all right," Pops said with a wry smile. "Told you the only way to put an end to this was to lure out that old grizzly bear," he quipped.

Corbin laughed in surprise. "Well, your spirits are certainly fine. You're a stubborn old man. I'll never hear the end of this one."

Pops cocked his ear. "How's that?"

"You were right." Corbin rolled his eyes. "But don't let it go to your head."

"Just call him Jack Reacher," Zane said with a laugh. Then he grew serious, his eyes locking with Corbin's. "I'm not gonna lie. You had me worried there for a minute." He paused. "But you did good. Doug would be proud. Once a frog man, always a frog man."

Emotion balled in Corbin's throat as he swallowed. "Thanks," he said gruffly.

The radio crackled. Cannon walked over and picked it up. "Yep ... glad to hear it ... we're all good here... That was Blayze," he said a few seconds later. "Your grandmother and sister are doing fine. All has been quiet there."

Sirens sounded in the distance.

Wallace grunted. "Now the police come after the trouble's over. Figures."

Cannon smiled. "So, who wants to explain this?"

"I'd might as well do it," Corbin said, "the sheriff already hates me. I figure he'll just add this to the list."

"Go easy on Sheriff Hendricks," Wallace cautioned, "he's had a hard time since his wife passed and—" The rest of his sentence got cut off as he winced in pain.

"Let's get you to the hospital," Zane said.

"I'll be there shortly, as soon as I get this squared away with the police," Corbin assured him. He looked at Delaney who was staring at Hugh, a dazed expression on her pale face. She was in shock. He put an arm around her. "Let's get you inside where it's warm."

She nodded numbly.

When they got inside the cabin, she turned to face him. "Is Wallace going to be okay?"

He offered a reassuring smile. "Yes."

"Should we go to the hospital with him?"

"We will, as soon as we get everything sorted out. Meanwhile, Zane will be with him."

Her lips pressed together in a tight line as she nodded. "Thank you, for everything."

"No thanks necessary." He cupped her face. "I love you, Delaney Mitchell."

"I love you too." Tears wet her eyes. "Promise me that you'll never leave me."

"I promise," he whispered as his lips touched hers with the softness of a feather.

Her arms went around him as she pulled him close, clinging to him. Gratitude washed over him as he held this amazing woman in his arms. She'd been through so much heartache and yet she was still standing strong. Through the window, he caught a glimpse of the sun, which had risen to its full height, shining brightly in an azure sky.

"Look, it's going to be a beautiful day," he proclaimed.

Delaney turned to look, a smile touching her lips. "Yes, I'm glad the last of the clouds have finally gone away."

EPILOGUE

Six months later ...

The roar of the crowd flowed like lightning through Delaney's veins as she looked out over the packed audience. Tonight's concert in Nashville was the final stop of her tour. Fitting that the tour would end in the very town where she'd gotten her start. Her new album *Transformation* had taken off, catapulting her to stardom. And no surprise, her song *Absolutely* spent two months in the number one slot and was still topping the charts.

"You'll recognize this next song from my upcoming album. It's called *The Lure of the Bear*."

Applause thundered through the arena.

She smiled in appreciation, holding up a hand to quiet the crowd. "This song is very special to me and is dedicated to my future father-in-law Wallace Spencer, who happens to be here tonight."

She looked at the front row where Wallace and Addie were sitting. "Give it up, folks, for my amazing family." The applause died down as she strummed her guitar, the familiar lyrics flowing like water from her lips. When she sang the last note, she laughed as the crowd cheered. "But wait ... there's more!" She held up her left hand to display the large rock on her ring finger. "The rumors are true. In a few days, I'm getting married to the most amazing man on the planet, who happens to be my bodyguard." She looked over to the edge of the stage where Corbin was standing.

A wicked grin curved her lips as she motioned. "Come on out here."

He frowned, shaking his head *no*, his lips drawing into a tight line.

"Aw, come on," she urged. "I wanna show you off. Cor—bin," she began chanting, pumping her fist in the air. The crowd followed her lead. A second later, his name boomed through the arena.

Finally, he strode out and stood by her side. "You're in so much trouble," he whispered, amusement stirring in his eyes.

She put an arm around his waist so he couldn't escape. "I wrote this next song about Corbin." She looked sideways at him, wiggling her eyebrows. "So, it's only fitting that he sings it with me. Don't you agree?"

"Yeah!" rustled through the crowd.

He laughed nervously. "You wouldn't."

A smile stretched over her lips. "Oh, but I would."

"All right," he finally said.

"Did you hear that, folks? He said *yes*."

"Under one condition," Corbin added.

"What's that?"

"That I get to do this." In a swift movement, he turned her to face him. His arms slid around her waist as he dipped her back, giving her a long, breathless kiss.

The crowd went wild, but Delaney hardly heard it over the roaring in her own ears as she got lost in the feel of his lips.

When the kiss was over, he set her back on her feet. She stumbled slightly as he reached to steady her. "Wow," she said quietly.

He grinned, his eyes dancing with a challenge as he leaned in and murmured in her ear. "So, Delaney Mitchell ... are you ready for all that lies ahead?"

It was a perfect evening. Her heart soared; a tidal wave of

complete and utter love washed over her as she peered into his mesmerizing eyes and saw the promise of many more perfect evenings to come. "Absolutely," she chimed joyously.

YOUR FREE BOOK AWAITS ...

Hey there, thanks for taking the time to read *The Reckless Warrior*. If you enjoyed it, please take a minute to give me a review on Amazon. I really appreciate your feedback, as I depend largely on word of mouth to promote my books.

The Reckless Warrior is a stand-alone novel, but you'll also enjoy more of Jennifer's books in the Navy SEAL Romance Series. Here's the order:

The Resolved Warrior - FREE
The Reckless Warrior
The Diehard Warrior
Jennifer's newest Navy SEAL Romance is coming soon!

To receive updates when more of my books are coming out, sign up for my newsletter at http://jenniferyoungblood.com/

If you sign up for my newsletter, I'll give you one of my books, Beastly Charm: A contemporary retelling of beauty & the beast, for FREE. Plus, you'll get information on discounts and other freebies. For more information, visit:

http://bit.ly/freebookjenniferyoungblood

ALSO BY JENNIFER YOUNGBLOOD

Check out Jennifer's Amazon Page:
   http://bit.ly/jenniferyoungblood

Georgia Patriots Romance
   The Hot Headed Patriot
   The Twelfth Hour Patriot

O'Brien Family Romance
   The Impossible Groom (Chas O'Brien)
   The Twelfth Hour Patriot (McKenna O'Brien)
   Rewriting Christmas (A Novella)
   Yours By Christmas (Park City Firefighter Romance)
   Her Crazy Rich Fake Fiancé

Navy SEAL Romance
   The Resolved Warrior
   The Reckless Warrior
   The Diehard Warrior

The Jane Austen Pact

Seeking Mr. Perfect

Texas Titan Romances

The Hometown Groom

The Persistent Groom

The Ghost Groom

The Jilted Billionaire Groom

The Impossible Groom

The Perfect Catch (Last Play Series)

Hawaii Billionaire Series

Love Him or Lose Him

Love on the Rocks

Love on the Rebound

Love at the Ocean Breeze

Love Changes Everything

Loving the Movie Star

Love Under Fire (A Companion book to the Hawaii Billionaire
Series)

Kisses and Commitment Series

How to See With Your Heart

Angel Matchmaker Series

Kisses Over Candlelight

The Cowboy and the Billionaire's Daughter

Romantic Thrillers

False Identity

False Trust

Promise Me Love

Burned

Contemporary Romance

Beastly Charm

Fairytale Retellings (The Grimm Laws Series)
Banish My Heart **(This book is FREE)**
The Magic in Me
Under Your Spell
A Love So True

Southern Romance
Livin' in High Cotton
Recipe for Love

The Second Chance Series
Forgive Me (Book 1)
Love Me (Book 2)

Short Stories
The Southern Fried Fix

ABOUT THE AUTHOR

Jennifer loves reading and writing clean romance. She believes that happily ever after is not just for stories. Jennifer enjoys interior design, rollerblading, clogging, jogging, and chocolate. In Jennifer's opinion there are few ills that can't be solved with a warm brownie and scoop of vanilla-bean ice cream.

Jennifer grew up in rural Alabama and loved living in a town where "everybody knows everybody." Her love for writing began as a young teenager when she wrote stories for her high school English teacher to critique.

Jennifer has BA in English and Social Sciences from Brigham Young University where she served as Miss BYU Hawaii in 1989. Before becoming an author, she worked as the owner and editor of a monthly newspaper named *The Senior Times*.

She now lives in the Rocky Mountains with her family and spends her time writing and doing all of the wonderful things that make up the life of a busy wife and mother.

For more information:
www.jenniferyoungblood.com
authorjenniferyoungblood@gmail.com

facebook.com/authorjenniferyoungblood

twitter.com/authorjenn1

instagram.com/authorjenniferyoungblood

Made in the USA
Coppell, TX
31 August 2023

21008952R00132